GOD ON TRIAL

A SHORT FICTION

BY

SABRI BEBAWI

BOOKS BY SABRI BEBAWI

In Love with a Married Woman
Tango under the Moon Light
A Dream Is Just That
Imagine
Consider the Following (series)

In memory of my guardian angel,
the Honorable Abbas Alaei.

ACKNOWLEDGMENTS

Thanks go to my muse Marisela, my family, and all the children from whom I acquire immense knowledge: Christian, Daniel, Bahareh, Sebastian, Richard, Alondra, Nardeen, Maria, and all the children of the world. Also to my dearest friends who impact my existence: Safwat, Androula, Shahnaz, Lina, Laila, Ginny, Atef, Celine and Terran, Dan, Dr. Hanson, and Professor Kathleen, and all the others whose names are printed in my heart. Also to Ronni and Richard Gates, who have buttressed and strengthened me for almost twenty years.

Thank you to my physicians, especially Grammy Award–winner Dr. Mike Vasilomanolakis, Dr. David Shen, Dr. David Rosenberg, Dr. Nancy Godfrey, Dr. Thomas Asciuto, and Dr. Linda Kaplan. Also to all my nurses and to victims of medical challenges.

ABOUT THE AUTHOR

The middle of five children, Sabri Bebawi was born in 1956 in the town of Fayoum, Egypt, where he attended law school at Cairo University. He then left Egypt for the United Kingdom. He was invited by Oxford University, where he spent some time, and never returned to Egypt. A few years later, after living and working in England, Italy, France, and Cyprus, he took refuge in the country he loved most, the United States.

In California he studied communications at California State University, Fullerton, then obtained a master's degree there in English education. Later he worked at many colleges and universities teaching English as a second language, freshman English, journalism, and educational technology. He did further graduate work at UCLA and obtained a PhD in education and distance learning from Capella University.

Although English is his third language, he has published many works in English on eclectic topics. It has always been his ambition to write novels, and this is his first attempt. As English is a foreign language to him, the task of writing a novel has been challenging.

As a child, Bebawi struggled to make sense of religions and their contradictions; in fact he grew up terrified of the word *God*. As he grew older and studied law, as well as all the holy books, he developed a more pragmatic and sensible stance; the word became just that—a word.

*"Is man one of God's blunders,
or is God one of man's blunders?"*

—*Friedrich Nietzsche
(1844–1900), German-Swiss philosopher and writer*

FORWARD

LISA BROWN-GILBERT

It is plausible to blame God for the abuses and ills that we may suffer in life, especially when it comes to the acts of those that follow the tenants and texts of religious worship. *God on Trial*, which is a dramatic fictional work by author Sabri Bebawi, not only addresses this question but also takes a delving look into the issue, from an interesting but disconcerting angle. Portrayed through the actions, thoughts, and circumstances of the protagonist – an unnamed 57-year-old English Professor and mediocre writer -who suffers from initially, undiagnosed schizophrenia. Finding himself at odds with the conditions of the world around him, He takes steps to start proceedings to impeach God in the

International Court of Human Rights. He intended to prove his case by compiling a manuscript titled "The Indictment of God" filled with adverse religious doctrine inclusive of the three major faiths Judaism, Catholicism [Christianity] and Islam. He determined that it was God's fault the abuses and miserable conditions of man exist, including his own suffering. He saw God as the provocateur of such conditions by virtue of writings contained in various Holy books. He saw God much like a mafia boss - he gives the orders through various religious doctrines but does not get his hands dirty.

He suffered through a rough childhood filled with numerous stressors; repeated illness, sexual abuse, a father lost to his vices, conflicts within family, government and religious institutions, and anxiety brought on by religious contentions (he was raised a Coptic Christian but forced to embrace the Islamic faith). Moreover, with repeated exposure to the most catastrophic sections of the Bible and the Quran, it created within him an unhealthy fear of God from a young age. His suffering through these issues seemed to lend towards his illness running rampant within him until, he began to portray dangerous outward signs of his disorder. Because, schizophrenia, affects the way a person thinks, feels and interacts with the world, this caused him to often lose touch with reality.

Remaining immersed in his deluded abyss, he often interacted with people aloud in public, that did not exist, such as the lawyer, Juliana he requested assistance from, in order to prepare his case against god.

For the protagonist, things spiral so completely out of control that the lines between reality and his world become completely obscured leading to his wife being murdered, and ultimately his own demise as well. In an ironic twist, his grieving sister pays a loving tribute to him by picking up where he left off, pursuing the case against God.

This novel is a realistic depiction of the sad human condition that is the world today, as well as a heart-wrenching depiction of one human's condition - the result of his contact with the people of God's world. Overall, I found this to be a good read that held my interest; it presented a controversial subject matter in a unique way and contained some thought provoking points, about faith, worship and

FORWARD

God. *God on Trial* is an out of the ordinary read that has great potential and I would recommend this book to readers that are looking to clarify the connection between the current state of the world and worshipping God.

INTRODUCTION

Most of us have an inner child. Some of us, though, ignore that inner child, suppress him, and bury him. Those of us who do are not free. They are forever imprisoned in a world of repressed memories of a time long past.

This time that some of us believe is long past is not in the past at all. Each of us is nothing but a collection of memories and experiences. These long-gone memories and experiences shape who we are as adults.

Some of these memories and experiences come back to life at some point in our adulthood. For some of us, they become vivid and real. At times they even form our reality as adults.

For some of us, theses long-ago experiences, especially if they aren't pleasant, or are in regard to our physical or mental health, never leave us, and we become doomed to relive them again and again on daily basis.

Indeed we are all victims of our own past and of our own minds and thoughts. Thoughts come to our consciousness from unknown sources; they come and leave each of us wondering, *Where the hell did that thought came from?*

For these reasons, it is not wise to judge one another; one does not, and cannot, know what another is feeling, thinking, or experiencing. We each interpret the world around us differently, and these interpretations depend greatly on the experiences and memories each of us keeps. That is why each of us is unique.

Religions have failed miserably in their attempt to explain our existence or who we really are. Philosophy has never ceased trying. Plato was concerned with the ultimate reality and believed reality doesn't exist in the real world. He believed this world we live in is a mere imitation of the real world. He never believed in the physical world and taught us not to trust it. In essence he taught us that our souls (if there is such a thing as a soul) are held captive by our bodies.

Philosophers, especially Plato, have pointed out to us that the conflicts and tensions within us are not in harmony. We can be serene only if we can bring harmony to these conflicts and tensions. Who among us can do that?

Aristotle, on the other hand, focused on the existence of a soul, without which we are incomplete. This writer finds no solace in either explanation.

The focus of this short novel is to present a series of occurrences, episodes, and experiences that create a surprising plot. Hypocrisy and duplicity, religious fervor and vehemence, corruption and depravity, wickedness and exploitation are the essence of the protagonist's world. In essence, and paradoxically, the protagonist abruptly finds himself mysteriously but figuratively in the unknown world of which some of us with psychological disorders are bewilderingly familiar.

There is a fine—very fine indeed—line between what is real and what is not. This line can easily and unconsciously be crossed. Once it is crossed, our world becomes what the great physicist and author Stephen Hawking debates, a mere possibility. All things are mere possibilities.

INTRODUCTION

This short novel addresses that. The protagonist lives in a world of his own, a creation of his mind. His antagonist is out of the realm of reality. A major threat and obstacle turns the protagonist's life inside out and upside down.

No moral judgment is made. This book is only a reflection of the human condition and takes a deeper look, using fictional characters, at it. With this novel, I do not intend to insult or defame any faith, religion, or belief.

CHAPTER ONE:

THE BEGINNING

There's that tormenting feeling again—a feeling he at times ignores; other times he descends into deep thoughts of yesterdays. He has grown so familiar with such disquieting emotions that occasionally he isn't even aware.

The most amazing thing, he ponders, is the inner child's mind, thoughts, and hunches the inner child that resides peacefully in all of us that many of us ignore. He, however, doesn't ignore it. He recognizes, respects, and nourishes his inner child.

He remembers. Though more than five decades have passed, it appears as though it were only last month, or at the risk of romanticizing history, last week. Yet it has been, indeed, more than five decades ago.

He was born in 1956 and raised in the exotic, confused, and utterly blurred world of Egypt. He was raised in an affluent family in a small oasis in Middle Egypt called Fayoum. The name originates from the word *efiom*, from the Coptic, the original Egyptian language, and means "the sea." Fayoum is sixty-three miles southwest of Cairo, the Egyptian capital.

He grew up in a family of five siblings. His father was a prominent criminal and constitutional barrister. He also was a functional alcoholic and an avid gambler, and publically branded as a philanderer.

Notwithstanding his father's eccentricities, he grew up with all his needs and wants met. His father was still a great, honorable gentleman in a time when there were gentlemen on our beautiful planet.

His mother was an ordinary housewife who afforded her children love in abundance. He and his siblings had learned manners, discipline, and etiquette since infancy. His mother was the warmest and kindest of mothers; her compassion and love were unconditional.

That perturbing feeling comes again with vivid memories that are graphic and distinct. He isn't sure whether he's awake or asleep. He sees and converses with the child in him. The child is only four years old. Then he is five, then six, then seven. He senses the continuity, the consistency, and the permanence.

He is feeling unwell. He is always not well.

What is wrong, son? How are you feeling? he hears his mother ask, just as she always has each time he is stricken by some bizarre illness.

"I am not well, Mom. I cannot move. I have a headache, and I want to vomit," he confusingly replies in a loud voice that startles him, for he hears himself. Now he is certain he is awake, or at least semi-awake. He is conversing with someone in the room, though he is alone, lying in bed in a semiconscious state.

He feels her; as she does each time he is sick, she gently checks his fever by inserting a long, strange-looking instrument into his rectum. The oddest thing is that he actually feels the thermometer being inserted into his rectum right now.

Oh! Lord Jesus, the Virgin Mary—your temperature is very high, son.

His mother's voice rings in his ears. He plainly feels her check his reddish, feverish body. He hears her scream. *We need to call Dr. Manoli right now.*

Ah! Dr. Manoli, he reminiscences. Dr. Manoli was a Greek citizen, one who managed—and no one knows how—to avoid President Gamal Abdel Nasser's order to deport all foreigners from Egypt and seize their businesses, properties, and assets. Dr. Manoli was a short, semi heavy man with a bald head, small eyes, and a bulging abdomen. He spoke Arabic with a Greek accent but was clearly understood. He was the family's doctor and often visited whenever needed.

His thoughts leap into a different direction, one unrelated to his illness. The name "Dr. Manoli" makes him remember his neighbors Yolanda and her old mother the night before they were to be deported to Greece by order of the Egyptian government. His mother, grandmother, and other people he can't recall were gathered around Yolanda and her mother, trying to comfort them over tea. The government had seized their villa, and they were to leave the next morning with nothing but their clothes. He remembers how sad that evening was. He sees tears flowing from Yolanda's eyes. He remembers her young beauty, her unique accent, and her long, blonde hair that made her face appear sensual and her lips kissable.

He mumbles, "Damn politics, damn government, damn Egypt."

In his state of semiconsciousness, he is unable to understand why the government took Yolanda's father's successful metal shop, seized their only residence, and forced them to depart the place they'd known for years. He feels heaviness in his heart, and his body shakes in sudden movements.

He sighs. His reminiscences rewind back to the situation at hand. He glances through the bedroom door and sees his mother pick up, as she has always done, the old black phone from a dark-brown table in a corner of the salon. She rolls the hand crank, and his father gets on the other end from his office.

Call Dr. Manoli to come immediately, his mother says. *The middle one is very sick. He has a rash all over his body, a fever, and a stiff neck, and he says he wants to vomit. He can't walk. My baby can't walk.*

She hangs up the phone, and fifteen to twenty minutes later, the doorbell rings.

Zakia, the nanny, opens the door and announces, *Madam, Dr. Manoli is here.*

Let him in, Zakia. Thanks to the angels of God. Blessed be the virgin, his mom utters.

The doctor comes to his bed. He takes his stethoscope and other strange medical instruments out of his doctor's bag and starts to examine him.

It all seems so real to him. He is still lying on his bed alone in his room, but in his thoughts, he is not alone. Everything happens in real time. The child in him is creative, imaginative, and in a more subtle way, visionary.

Dr. Manoli listens to his heart; he checks his body all over; he asks him to open his mouth wide and stick his tongue out. The doctor inserts something wooden and long into his mouth that makes him gag. He tells the doctor about his nausea, headache, and overall ailment. He sees gloom over the doctor's face; he notices worry in his mother's demeanor; and he sees fright in Zakia's eyes. Though he might be aware this happened more than five decades ago, the experience is actual and tangible. He is now confused and fairly terrified.

Dr. Manoli puts his instrument back in his bag and asks the mother to go outside with him so he can speak with her. He hears his mom cry loudly, and both Zakia and Dr. Manoli are trying to comfort her.

It's baffling to him. How can an event that happened five decades ago become so alive and real? He is certain, and his adult medical examinations prove, that this childhood illnesses, including meningitis, left him scarred for life.

He now knows he is awake. He is neither dreaming nor hallucinating; he is merely reliving yesterdays. He is experiencing one of his unceasing trances. Fatigue and exhaustion of all this déjà vu" takes him out of his trance, and for a very short time, he falls asleep.

In his sleep state, he recalls his religious mother praying nonstop to the angels, to the Virgin Mary, and to all saints. Some of these saints he knows about; others he does not. His mother has always believed, until this moment, that his survival was a direct result of her prayers.

His inseparable companion, insomnia, shakes him hard enough to awaken him. He's now fully awake again. He gets up, walks to his desk, and lights one of his Dunhill cigarettes. He wonders why he goes in and out of these unusual reveries.

CHAPTER TWO:

ANXIETY

He is now five decades and seven. He has the demeanor of a strong-willed man whose pragmatism almost always overshadows any emotions he experiences. He is married to a beautiful young girl named Sofia who had been his English student twenty years ago. She went back to Rome and they both lost contact for years. He miraculously met her again, through some mutual friends, on one of his many visits to Rome only three years ago. Sofia is deeply in love with him and she is always preoccupied by his wellbeing and his health. She is twenty years his junior; a pretty Italian with a charming oval face adorned by long dark soft hair that makes her femininity shine. Her reddish full lips make her adorable and desirable. She has big brown eyes that often sparkle with a tear or two for him. She is slim and tall, but not too tall. Her smile is always a comfort for him; his world lightens up when he sees her smile. Her laughter echoes in his ears as a most sensuous melody. He is a very lucky man to have Sofia in his life.

His sister, Savana, is the only sibling he has in the USA. She is ten years younger than he is, married and lives with her husband. She lives near him, so she visits him sometimes to check on him and ensures that Sofia does not need help attending to his ailing health. Although Savana is a busy pianist, she makes effort to see her brother as often as she can.

Though he's an English teacher, he carries himself as if he were a public prosecutor. Though he's feeble, he never admits his frailty. In secrecy he confronts his meagerness, and everyone around him sees him as robust and even, bizarrely enough, athletic. He and any kind of sport, however, have never been compatible. At times he takes walks along the beach with a mind bombarded by thoughts that he's never able to hear the sound of the waves or even see the seagulls hovering above his head or the little birds trudging by his feet

What happens in one's childhood never goes away; adulthood is affected in every way, not merely psychological but—more significantly—physical. This is part of the mockery of life.

Childhood dilemmas manifest themselves once again in his old age. First it was heart glitches, then it was cancer. In sync with life's absurdity, it doesn't stop there.

On a warm June evening at about six o'clock, he's having a pleasant dinner and wine with a dear friend at *Le Comptoir du Panthéon* in Paris. The restaurant is located next to the *Pantheon* and offers a wonderful view of it; he sits on the terrace, so he has a good view of the Eiffel Tower and the Sorbonne. The place is bustling with locals as well as tourists. He has the soup of the day and the pan-seared fish, which is heavenly. He and his friend share a bottle of exquisite Bordeaux. They both appreciate high-quality wine, and Bordeaux can be fine.

That Saturday day of June second is quite uneventful for him, since he visits Paris often, and he lived there in his long-lost youth. Earlier that day he went to Jardin de Luxembourg and also walked along the Seine. He had lunch at the famous Le Fouquet's.

He has always felt restless about the appalling changes that globalization has imposed upon his beautiful Paris. Today he was somewhat mortified by some of the scenes on Rue de Champs-Élysées; in essence he is not quite himself at dinner at *Le Comptoir du Panthéon*. Earlier that day, he saw many Gypsies trying to rob tourists using their mischievous techniques of pretending to be disabled or using babies as props; he saw many Arab men in Islamic clothing and Arab women depicting thirteenth century era; and he saw many unscrupulous youth who seemed to intend on causing mayhem. Paris has not been the same.

After finishing his dinner, he is relaxing and discussing current affairs with his friend while sipping his Bordeaux. In Paris, as well as in most of Europe, tables at restaurants are very close to one another. As he sits in his chair with his wineglass in his right hand, his left hand resting on the arm of the chair, and his legs crossed, he suddenly and involuntarily extends his right leg in a strong unexplained jerk and kicks the bottom of the chair next to him; in the chair, a large gentleman is sitting as he chats with his group of friends. Understandably the gentleman angrily gets up and utters, "What the fuck!" The incident is terrifying and astonishing. At that moment he imagines returning to California with a black eye and a concussion. His face turns yellow; his body is shaking; he is petrified at what just happened.

Fearing the large gentleman, he explains that he has no idea why his leg jerked in such a way and apologizes. The large gentleman recognizes the shock and fear and allows the matter to settle. The gentleman sits down again, and so does he, and he, being the coward he is, is grateful his bones are still intact.

Though how his leg moved so violently and involuntarily is confusing, he doesn't make much of the incident.

Life's ludicrousness never ceases. He leaves for Bergamo, Italy, about an hour's drive from Milan. Monaco, Venice, and Bergamo are the greatest places he has ever visited. He and his companions are dining at La Marianna, located in a centuries-old building at the west end of Città Alta. This family-run restaurant has a limited but regularly changing menu of local dishes.

He is sitting at a well-decorated table; to his right locals are standing at the bar, drinking and chatting. The old and romantic Italian music is intriguing, and the atmosphere is breathtaking. Patrons are happy, conversing, drinking, and swinging to the music. The restaurant is well decorated with classical paintings, colorful chandeliers, beautifully set round tables and a water fountain in the middle. In front of him is a balcony filled with gorgeous flowers; beneath it are seven tables that seat four people each. Behind him is a stunning garden filled with daffodils, calla lily, carnations, orchids, and daisies flowers in all colors: burgundy, rouge, pink, yellow, red, and white—all the colors of life for those of us who are alive. He sees mountains, scattered with green plants, on the other side of the garden.

He orders the tastiest wine on the wine list to savor over appetizers. For his main course he orders *casoncelli alla bergamasca* (stuffed pasta) and a *filetto ai ferri* (grilled filet of beef).

The elegant waiter, who was about twenty-five-years-old and pleasingly graceful and stylish in appearance and manner, arrives with the bottle of Chianti and pours a glass of the wine for him. Suddenly, as he reaches for the glass, his right hand involuntarily extends in a stretched motion, hitting the glass and sending it flying toward the table next to him. In shame and confusion, he covers his face with his palms; everyone is in disbelief, as is he. No apology is sufficient to ease the astonishment. It is only then that he realizes something is dreadfully amiss.

Everyone is apologizing to everyone, and confusion ensues. The waiter calls upon someone to come and clean the mess his customer just created. A girl at the table next to him has wine all over her dress; fortunately it's a reddish dress. Her companions take out their handkerchiefs and attempt to clean the wine off her pretty, elegant gown. He isn't sure whether they're smiling or frowning. He's out of the moment and in his head.

What the fuck is going on? he wonders.

He tries to forget and emerge himself in the beautiful music that is playing; the music lifts his spirit and takes him into his memories. He remembers the time when he lived in Italy long ago. He relives several events, conversing in his thoughts with old forgotten friends he hasn't seen in years.

He carefully watches and analyzes the patrons around him. Flowers merge with their faces, and the pretty maidens' hair becomes golden and their bodies transparent. It's as though he's in a museum filled with nudes. This is his way of dealing with his unusual dilemma.

He and his companions take a taxi and leave for the hotel. In his hotel room, he prepares for his trip to Como the next morning. All his friends are excited, while he's thinking about his involuntary, violent leg and arm movements.

His fears and confusion bring him back earlier than planned to Long Beach, California, where he lives. Throughout the rest of the year, he experiences some sudden leg and arm movements, for which he visits several neurologists. He is diagnosed with what the doctors call "myoclonic *seizures.*"

His condition has become more and more confusing. His legs and hands often move violently and involuntarily, and his fingers twitch. He also experiences tremors throughout his body. The symptoms begin to take different forms, and the attacks occur at different times. Neither he nor his close friends have a clue as to what these involuntary movements mean. They're confusing, alarming, and somewhat sidesplitting. His intellect, demeanor, and sense of mental control have been gradually diminishing.

Being the stubborn person he has always been, however, these seizures do not stop him from doing what he loves to do—travel. The following year, in July, he goes to Venice, Italy, with a group of friends. Ah! Venice, Venice! What an incredibly fascinating place. In his youth, more than thirty years ago, he visited Venice many times. How strange, he thinks, that when one is young, one does not appreciate beauty or elegance in the same way that one does in advanced age. Many writers have attempted to describe what Venice is, but he is almost certain that no writer can truly capture it.

He and his friends arrive at the train station in Venice, and in front of them is the pier. They take a boat from pier eighty-two for only two stops to Hotel Lanterna di Venezia in the Rialto area. They disembark and, following the directions they have, turn right and pass several well-known shops. During the walk he tries to grasp the beauty of Venice all at once. He feels this is a surreal moment, as he experienced the same feelings each time he visited Venice in the 1970s and 1980s.

At the hotel, they are greeted by Lucia, a beautiful young Italian woman who is warm, friendly, helpful, and of course deliciously sexy. Lucia takes the group to their rooms; how he wishes she could stay with him in the room.

After he settles and freshens up, he walks to the famous Piazza San Marco, which is heavily populated with tourists. He goes to a restaurant and sits at a bar for drinks and hors d'oeuvres; he's quite surprised this restaurant in particular has a special cover charge for listening to music. Amazingly the band plays for ten to fifteen minutes, then goes to the bar next door to play for ten to fifteen minutes, then comes back.

He has a wonderful time reminiscing and tapping his foot to the music while enjoying his Chianti. Afterward he walks back to the hotel in the warm Venice night. He chats for a short while with his friends then goes to bed. As soon as he lies down, however, his legs begin to move, then his hands, then—for the first time—his whole body. He sinks into a trance and doesn't know for certain whether he is asleep.

* * *

He's now back home in California. It is another night. That tantalizing sensation overtakes his natural senses again. Growing up, he always felt a sense of discomfort that was unrelated to his illnesses, and he still feels it now. He never has been able to identify the source of his severe and unusual discomfort. He wonders whether it was his family, religion in general, or society, with its unscrupulous culture.

He thinks of his parents. "Sadly, They were at odds," he hears himself utter. "And rightfully so."

His mother was at home, taking care of five kids, and his father was either working or endlessly playing. His mother had a tender soul. She was simple, affectionate, and caring, and loved her children dearly. The child in him sees her before him as a pretty young woman with fair skin, brown hair, and large brown eyes. She stands by his bed; she is neither too tall nor too short and neither too slim nor too heavy, but she is mysterious. Though his mother probably never knew it, she has had an immense impact on his life that continues with him until this moment of certain hallucination.

He becomes fully awake. It is 2:25 a.m. He gets up and decides to make a cup of espresso forte. After breaking a couple of coffee cups, spilling coffee all over his kitchen counter and floor, and mumbling a few expletives, he cleans up. Now he is calm; now he will taste the fruit of his coffee-making adventure; he places the cup on his desk and starts to write.

> *I'm not sure my parents' odd relationship had any effect on me. I was a happy child tormented by religion and religious people's hallucinations. I was tormented by Egyptian hypocrisy. I've seen a great deal of hypocrisy, child abuse, infidelity, abuse of women, and abuse by the government, churches, and mosques.*

He hears the voice of his mother; during his childhood she always read to him in bed before he went to sleep. Now she reads from the Bible. In both her wisdom and lack of awareness, she reads from the Book of Genesis and the Book of Revelations.

This exposure to apocalyptic writing at a very young age has had a profound effect on him.

Being imaginative, and in this phantasmagoric state, he now experiences the same fright he experienced as a child. He returns to bed and suddenly falls asleep but is soon awoken by one of his many epileptic seizures. His body shakes uncontrollably, and his tremors seem to have a mind of their own.

As his attack gradually dissipates, he thinks of the savagery of God and questions why a peaceful God would be so cruel and nasty. These thoughts make him feel even more terrified. Since childhood he has been petrified of that entity referred to as "God."

At age seven or eight, he developed an obsessive-compulsive disorder. He'd repeat the phrase "God forgive me" to himself all day until he went to bed. He kept this a secret because he had no idea how his mother, siblings, or Zakia would react. He remembers that he often went to Zakia, who was a Muslim, and asked her to hold him. She would oblige, and he would feel protected, even from that savage God.

He gets out of bed. It is 3:42 a.m. He makes another cup of espresso forte and sits at his desk, thinking. Again he writes.

This phase simply shaped my feelings about whether God does indeed exist. I often thought I'd be better than him or her or it, for I would not be as cruel, brutal, or malicious. Today I am an agnostic, and I can't get myself to understand why anyone would believe in such a God as depicted in the holy books, including the Bible.

In addition to the Bible, there were other sources of great damage. Egypt is an Islamic country. I was exposed to and forced to learn about Islam and its holy book, the Quran, which is like the Bible in its catastrophic content. I was forced to learn about the Islamic laws, Sharia, even though I was a Coptic. I did so in schools, and I did so in everyday affairs. I was even forced to memorize and recite verses from the Quran, which also had a negative impact on me.

The daily prayers announced over loudspeakers, and coming from all directions, were a frightening experience for me. Everywhere in Egypt, between each mosque there is a mosque, and even that wasn't enough. The radio broadcasted Quran readings repeatedly. Even today the memory of these sounds brings a deep downheartedness to my soul.

I remember Sheikh Omar Abdel-Rahman, the blind cleric who's in a North Carolina prison now for conspiring to commit terrorism. His mosque was right behind our house. I remember Abdel-Rahman's Friday sermons. He'd curse the Christians, Jews, and Americans (I don't know why he cursed Americans) publically over a loud-speaker that echoed miles away. The sheikh would scream in a screeching, deafening voice, "May God burn them and displace their children, and may God burn their houses." The congregation would repeat, "Amen." And the pattern would continue.

This persisted for a long time. We were so used to it, however, that it didn't bother us much. The amazing thing is that Sheikh Abdel-Rahman was a friend of my father's. He often visited my father at his law firm and spent hours talking with him. My father considered him a harmless, kind man.

Well, for once my father was wrong. The sheikh always has been a terrorist, and he put his evil spirit into action. Fortunately he's in prison now. I hope he never gets out.

He stops writing for a minute and wonders how the United States allowed that savage man to enter this country. Where was American intelligence? Didn't they know how radical Abdel-Rahman was? This was simply bizarre. But the United States government overlooks such things so often that he wonders whether the word *intelligence* is fitting at all.

His mind is racing, and he grows exhausted with the burden of thoughts. Hoping for a few minutes of sleep, he goes back to bed. His hope materializes, or perhaps he thinks so; at the very least, he is semi-asleep.

CHAPTER THREE:

A WORLD IN TURMOIL

Another night of unrest looms; his mind battles with disordered thoughts and considerations. This time it takes him to a roller coaster of seizures. Just as he recovers from one, another begins. He is petrified and agitated, but he is not afraid of death; he welcomes it anytime. He is horrified of losing the most precious thing he has ever had—his mind.

He gets up and walks around his small apartment. He stands by the window, watching the water in the bay; it is calm, and the sky is clear, with a few bright stars. The silence is deafening. He looks above the sky and wonders where the hell God is.

"He certainly has died, just as all things do," he mumbles. "Yes, he must be dead, or perhaps he is in a coma, since he sees nothing, hears nothing, and certainly does nothing."

He moves away from the window and walks around aimlessly. It is close to four in the morning; he hasn't slept at all and feels tired and fossilized.

He goes to bed with a new feeling of anger— anger at the entity that created life, though he is certain it is neither a god nor a demon; he is simply enraged.

He lays his head on his pillow and focuses on sleep, as though he were trying to reach a level of hypnosis. He knows if he doesn't get a few hours of sleep, he'll start to hallucinate for real, as if he were not already.

Though many people count sheep to fall asleep, he counts the number of wars that have taken place before and after his birth. He thinks of the hungry children. He thinks of the wars between men and women. He thinks of evil and corruption across the planet. He is disappointed at the country he loves the most, the United States. He thinks of terrorists and their evil ways, killers and their cold blood, abusers and their wickedness, and he revisits America's blatant disregard for basic human decency and social responsibility.

He finally falls asleep. He doesn't know if he really is sleeping, as his mind continues to whirl.

He gets up, startled and horrified again. He has just seen two American marines walking through Domodedovo International Airport in Moscow; they face Edward Snowden, the man unfairly accused of simply telling the ugly truth about America's wrong-doings. They blindfold him and lay him down on a wooden structure. Then one of the marines beheads him with an Arabian sword. Blood is everywhere. People at the airport are going about their business, not caring or even noticing the horrifying scene.

The next scene he envisions is inexplicable. He sees a large number of skinheads, a group of priests and preachers, and faceless others holding large crosses, chanting, dancing, and shouting, "USA, USA, USA."

They are celebrating the beheading of Edward Snowden.

He swiftly gets up, his heart pounding, his body shaking, his eyes misting. He looks at his watch; it is

4:14 a.m. He hasn't had a continuous thirty minutes of sleep.

"Should I make a cup of espresso forte? Should I open a bottle of wine? Wine at four in the morning! This is insane." He talks loudly to himself and opts for neither.

He has an infrequent urge to write. He sits at his desk with no idea regarding what he wants to write. He scribbles a few words. Thoughts of his years in law school invade his mind. Perhaps it is because he feels he lives in a lawless world and certainly a lawless country.

Although I enjoyed my law study, I'm not sure whether it is now serving others or harming them. I spent four years at Cairo University's School of Law, a semester at Oxford University, and one year studying law in California. Many years of reading and training have certainly affected my character. The legal consciousness I've developed has caused me a great deal of grief.

I'm always unhappily aware of the lawlessness around me. Laws are abused around the globe, and only the rich and powerful are above the law. The director of national intelligence (or lack thereof) blatantly and deliberately, with no shame or remorse, lies to Congress, yet he walks freely, while Edward Snowden, who merely told the truth about illegal activities, has been stripped of his citizenship and has become a stateless fugitive.

In Egypt and the Arab world, raped girls and women who possess the courage to report such heinous crimes are routinely accused of prostitution and imprisoned in a shameless, lawless society.

Rupert Murdoch's wrongdoing in London is another disturbing affair. His journalists'

hacking the phones of innocent people showed a blatant disregard not only for decency but also— and more importantly—the law. The connection to British Prime Minister David Cameron was another slap in the face and a kick in the balls to those few of us who still have respect for the law. Evidently an aide to the culture minister, Jeremy Hunt, in Mr. Cameron's government, had a strong relationship with a lobbyist for Murdoch's News Corporation when the company was seeking full control of Britain's most lucrative broadcaster, British Sky Broadcasting.

Without question, the immoral, iniquitous beheadings that routinely take place in Saudi

Arabia—America's seductive, sexy mistress— are among the most barefaced violations of humanity and the law.

The governments of China, North Korea, and Russia, as well as most African countries,

consistently violate human rights and show indifference to laws, including international laws. Even worse are the United States and its Western allies' nonstop indictments of such indifference while they're just as apathetic and indifferent.

The most lawless of all countries is Mexico. Kidnappings, murders, drug trafficking, prostitution, and the unconcealed corruption of the authorities, which is is always under God's umbrella. —just like in the Middle East, where religious delusion is the norm and cultural delirium is a pattern.

He grows exhausted. It is almost 6:20 a.m. He must sleep. He has an 8:30 a.m. appointment with his neurologist. He gets up and goes to bed again, hoping he has gotten a bit of defeat out of his system.

As soon as he lies in bed, a seizure grips him for less than a minute. He smiles at the nature of man and thinks a little longer.

He tries to fall asleep, but his mind is still reeling, his body shaking. He thinks about getting up and walking for a while but decides against it. Sometime later he falls asleep—his normal sleep, which is not sleep at all.

CHAPTER FOUR:

THE PROSECUTOR

On rare occasions, he goes into a deep sleep. He doesn't know for certain if now is one of these rare occasions. In a semi dream state, he feels the needs to impeach God. He sees himself as a representative of the Office of the Prosecution. He is responsible for confirmation of charges in major world cases that concern international humanitarian law brought to the International Court of Justice. These include crimes against humanity, such as murder, rape, and sexual slavery; war crimes, such as acts of terrorism, murder, outrage upon personal dignity, torture, and savagery; and other violations of international humanitarian law, including the abuse of children and the enlistment of children into armed forces in many parts of the world.

For him there is a major challenge. How he will summon a nonexistent being to appear before a court of law? He resolves the issue by deciding the trial should be in absentia.

A slight earthquake, which is common in California, interrupts his trance. He now thinks of Edward Snowden and Julian Assange; a mysterious power is trying to prevent him from divulging the truth; it is trying to forbid him from exposing viciousness, savagery, fear.

It takes him a long time to settle. He's now certain he's fully awake because of the quake. He doesn't remember much of what he was thinking about minutes earlier. He remembers only something about a trial, the International Court of Justice, and crime and punishment.

He recalls Dostoevsky's classic novel *Crime and Punishment*. In the book a former student named Raskolnikov considers committing an unclear hideous crime. He's consumed with the idea of crime and punishment. He also is convinced God has committed repugnant crimes against humanity, and he intends, in his state of hallucination, to have him impeached.

His thoughts deplete him. He is severely tired and decides he should try to sleep. A few minutes he lies down, his body begins to shake, and another seizure takes him to another dimension of existence; he isn't sure which dimension or whether he exists at all. This seizure lasts about two minutes and leaves his mind drained and his fragile body floating in the unknown, not well understood world of Stephen Hawking, where the theme is "No matter how thorough our observation of the present, the past, like the future, is indefinite and exists only as a spectrum of possibilities." Everything is a mere possibility. He may not have had a seizure. He might not be thinking what he is thinking. His conviction to punish God for his crimes might be just a mere possibility and not necessarily fact.

Quel dommage! *Mere possibilities*, he muses. *If everything is a mere possibility*, he thinks, *then our own existence is only a possibility. Even the entity people refer to as "God" is a mere possibility.*

The prosecutor part of his personality takes over. *How will God appear before the court?* he wonders.

God cannot be summoned, for he has no land, no country, and no address. He is simply a mirage; he is an imagination, a creation of our own minds. Yet he is determined to bring God to justice; he needs answers.

The seizure he just experienced leaves him in a unique state; he doesn't know whether he's awake, asleep, or still under the spill of the seizure. He is aware of his thoughts, though. Some extraordinary power brings the child in him to life again. He decides to write down his thoughts.

The summer of 1967 has had a long-lasting impact on my personality and life. I was only a ten-year-old child. A ten-year-old child then was in no way like a ten-year-old child now. We were innocent; we knew little or nothing; we were utterly dependent, insecure, and timid. And I was no different.

The war began on June fifth, and we lived in darkness, amid the dreadful sounds of sirens.

When my mother left my father and us behind, my father took good care of us at first. Every day my two brothers and I ate at the best restaurants. My father showed us immense affection.

Then, for some reason, possibly out of fear and worry, he began to lock us in the house.

He'd take the key then he send for us when it was time to go eat. After we ate, he'd lock us up in the house again. I never forgot how my brothers and I felt like prisoners as we spoke to our neighbors from the balcony, veranda, or windows. It was an eerie time; it was a ghostly time. It was a time never to forget and a time to be engraved in our souls for eternity.

The unpredictable and volatile happened; my father became unable to care for us, so he made the vilest of decisions; he transferred my brothers and me to his father's mansion in a village called Tobhar so my grandmother and my uncle's wife could attend to us. It was a grave move, one that nearly destroyed me physically and mentally.

I hated the village, and that's possibly the reason why I don't like to be close to nature today; it brings about fear, discomfort, and unexplainable despair. I detested my grandfather's enormous mansion; it scared me so much that I would run from one area of the house to another. I despised my grandfather, as for the first time, I grasped who he was. He was a landowner and was severely abusive to the farmers who worked the plantation; I watched him whip them as though they were his slaves. He was abusive to everyone around him, including my grandmother. Yet he also was a very religious man and never missed Mass or Sunday communion.

He read the newspapers every morning and afternoon and repeatedly cursed President Gamal Abdel Nasser. Abdel Nasser had confiscated part of my grandfather's land during the revolution reforms and given it to farmers so they could care for and improve themselves. My grandfather hated this, as he was a heartless capitalist. Perhaps this is why I am now an earnest socialist.

My brothers and I, along with my four male cousins, slept in two large bedrooms, with two children in each bed. I slept next to my twenty-two-year-old cousin, George. Late at night I'd feel him take my hand and place it on his pubic hair; then he'd force me to hold his penis. At my age and in my innocence, I couldn't understand why that thing, his penis, was big, nor did I understand what my cousin wanted.

In fractions of a second, I'd recall how our young female helpers at home used to ask to see and touch my tiny penis and also ask me to touch their breasts and private parts. I must admit that I liked the sensation, even though I didn't understand it. This went on for a long time. We played doctor, and we played husband and wife. The helpers were teenagers, and I was a mere child with no understanding of this human pleasure.

Though I liked what had been going on with the helpers, I didn't like or understand what my cousin George was doing. He'd ask me to turn around and place his penis between my buttocks, and I'd lie there frightened and confused. A nagging voice inside me kept telling me that what was happening was wrong. I'd cry in silence, afraid to tell anyone. I was a ten-year-old child then, which is the equivalent, in terms of knowledge and innocence, of a three- or four-year-old today.

From June to July 1967, the abuse continued, and I loathed being in my grandfather's mansion. Then I became very ill. I was on the verge of death and constantly cried for my mother. Finally, against my grandfather's wishes, my grandmother ordered a car and transported me to my mother in Fayoum. Though I was terribly sick, I was the happiest soul in the world when I saw my mother, my maternal grandmother, and my baby sister, who was just a year or two old.

This happiness didn't come without a grave sense of guilt for having left behind my baby brother in the village. He was only seven years old, and God only knows what form of abuse he went through. He and I never have talked openly about it, although I told him everything that happened to me. I'd cry for him each night and beg my mother to call for him to join us.

As for my older brother, who sadly met his demise at the age of forty, I wasn't so worried. He was thirteen years old at the time, and he loved the village life and living in the mansion. He enjoyed climbing trees, playing in the lakes, and riding horses and camels. There was no reason for me—or at least I believed—to worry about him.

At my maternal grandmother's house, another male cousin, Magdy, who was twenty-five at the time, also sexually abused me. While my mother, grandmother, and baby sister were asleep, he'd force me to go to the toilet with him and touch his penis. Again I was terrified to tell anyone about these incidents.

After remembering all this, he's even more confused, and his mind feels even more muddled by Hawking's ideas about possibilities. He wonders whether any of those events really happened. He knows they did, but considering that all things are possible, it's also possible that they never happened. He convinces himself to fuck it and go to sleep, or at least try to.

He goes to bed, thinks a bit more about putting God on trial in absentia, and falls asleep.

CHAPTER FIVE:

IN ABSENTIA

It is 5:44 a.m. He's fully awake and attentive this morning. He makes his espresso forte and sits at his desk. He lights a Dunhill cigarette while waiting for his computer to start up. Once the computer is on, he checks his e-mails, replies to the ones that deserve attention, opens his web browser, and goes to CNN.com. His habit of reading CNN news is very much like alcoholism or drug addiction; he does it; he regrets it; and he swears he'll never do it again, but the next morning, he does it again with a great deal of remorse. The reason for this remorse is that he's developed an extraordinary disrespect for any American news and for many American journalists. To him they aren't reporting news; they're making news. He recalls Atef, his best friend, once referring to CNN as "CMM," which for him means "could be, might be, and maybe." He chuckles, thinking how accurate the name is. Having worked as a journalism professor at one point, he feels embarrassed for the whole profession in the United States. He prefers NPR, BBC, and France 24. Nevertheless he still reads CNN news religiously, even though he knows it's a very unhealthy, dangerous, and brain-frying substance.

He loses consciousness yet still functions. He's deeply focused on the trial. He's aware that a trial can take place without the accused being present. In essence it is clear that God, the accused, has waved his or her right to be present. He understands that a counsel appointed by the defense office can represent the accused. This is to guarantee that the accused's rights are not violated.

In his mirage he is deeply troubled; he doesn't know how he will bring God to trial or try it in absentia. Anglo-Saxon law, in its early days, would not allow any tribunal to enter a judgment on an accusation unless the accused was present. Such a rule was rooted in common law. His delusion takes him to the Romano-Germanic legal system. His hopes elevate.

He recalls the trial of Martin Bormann, the Nazi party secretary who was indicted, tried in absentia in 1946, and sentenced to death based on article twelve of the Charter of the International Military Tribunal.

He thinks about a recent case of trying in absentia, in which four suspects were tried for the brutal murder of Lebanese prime minister Rafic Hariri.

He now thinks of asking for assistance and goes through all the names he knows. This isn't an easy task. He needs someone with a legal background and above-average critical-thinking skills. He thinks of one lawyer friend who seems to be always next to him, talking to him and advising him and at times telling him how he should react to various situations. She appears next to him, as she often does.

Ah! Juliana Maigret?

Juliana Maigret is a forty-year-old attorney with a very strong disposition. She is a highly intelligent young woman; one can see that just by looking at her round shaped face and deep brown eyes. She is about 5'6" tall and does not weigh more than a hundred and twenty pounds. She carries her hair unusually short and carries herself with great confidence. Juliana has always been by his side.

Yes? Do you know what time it is? Juliana answers in a grouchy voice

Not really. What time is it? he politely replies.

It's fucking six in the morning. If this isn't about something important, I'll kick your ass, she semiseriously tells him.

She raises her head, then her upper body, and sits comfortably on the couch next to his desk, listening attentively.

Listen, he says, *I'm contemplating bringing God before the International Court of Justice.*

You fucking want to do what? Have you been drinking? Please tell me you did not say that.

We really shouldn't discuss this here, he tells her. *America is now a fourth-world country, and none of us is safe. We have people listening—the NSA, the CIA, the FBI, and even TBN; no one is safe. Let's meet at Simmzy's on Second Street in Belmont Shore. I can't drive now because of my seizures, so I'll walk there. OK? I'll tell you everything, then.*

D'accord. This had better be good. When do you want to meet? she says in a much calmer tone.

Tuesday at five thirty, if that works for you.
Oui, oui. OK. See you then.

She simply disappears. He feels a bit of relief and strongly feels he'll be able to try God in absentia. All it will take is some serious research, a well-drafted complaint to the International Court of Justice, and a great deal of luck.

* * *

It is now 6:46 a.m. He's worried that if he goes to bed, he'll suffer another seizure. He's tired of seizures because they drain his brain and make him lethargic and unable to think clearly. He needs all his intellect now, whatever is left of it, to accomplish his task.

He reflects until a few minutes after seven. He decides it's best for him to go to bed and wake up in a few hours so he can prepare for his discussion with Juliana Maigret tomorrow.

On a piece of paper, he scribbles "G-O-D," followed by "Juliana Maigret, Tuesday." Underneath it he writes, "I shall get you." Then he switches off his desk light and slowly and unsteadily walks to the bedroom, as though he were intoxicated, although he hasn't drunk any alcohol. He's intoxicated by his deep thoughts. He trudges until he reaches his bed. Then he throws his unstable body next to his wife Sofia, turns to his right side, and falls asleep.

He is in a restless sleep and is either dreaming or delirious; he doesn't know for sure. He thinks of about recruiting high-level detectives and seeking their input. He's thinking of whom he will call to the stand to testify.

"Pope Francis" is the first name that comes to his mind. *Yes*, he tells himself confidently. He thinks summoning the pope to testify is a clever strategy. Indeed the Catholic Church has a very dark history. Then he comes up with a witness from the Jewish faith and another representing the Islamic faith. For the Jews, he thinks he will summon Sephardi chief rabbi Shlomo Amar. For the Islamic faith, no one would be better than the grand imam of Al-Azhar, Ahmed el-Tayeb, in Cairo, Egypt. He thinks this will cover the three main sects that follow the principal three books inspired by God.

He feels a sense of contentment and can't wait to share his idea with Juliana on Tuesday evening. He

will tell her about the indictment. He will consult
with her about the approach. He is buoyant in his
phantasmagoric state.

His restlessness often keeps his wife on the alert.
Sofia is a tender, goodhearted woman. Her care for
him and his illnesses are unconditional. He adores
her; she is tall, slim, and has long dark hair that makes
her pretty, oval face shine under any circumstances.
She supports him in everything he does. When he
suffers from seizures, she holds him tightly and pro-
tects him. She handles his madness effectively and
is never bothered by his impotence. Her eyes often
speak volumes regarding her inner self. In light of his
vast experience with women, Sofia is the best of all.

He recalls how he knew Sofia. He met her many
years ago. She was an English student in one of his
classes at the local college. She was only twenty-one
years old then. She captured his attention instantly,
and they had a short fling that left an impact on him.
Then Sofia, for one reason or another, suddenly disappeared. He resigned himself to the fact that she
must have returned to Rome, where she is from.

She did indeed return to Rome. Many years later,
as he searched for her, as he had done for years,

he found her in Rome through friends, and they reconnected, this time for good. They reminisced, recalled, and laughed. Her laughter, which has never changed since she was twenty-one, is a source of energy for him. They married despite all of his challenges.

He shares all his thoughts with Sofia, even his intention to bring God to justice. She cautiously listens, her eyes showing that she feels his pain and anguish. He tells her about his meeting with Juliana Maigret. She's a bit puzzled, as she has never heard the name before. She reluctantly smiles and advises him to be careful sailing in such unchartered waters.

CHAPTER SIX:

TUESDAY WITH
MS. MAIGRET

It is 5:16 p.m. He dresses casually; says good-bye to Sofia, who knows nothing about what he does all day; leaves his apartment; and walks toward Simmzy's on Second Street. The meeting with Juliana is in fourteen minutes. He arrives, but she isn't there yet. He asks for a corner table so they can be away from the noise and avoid being overheard. He sits down and anxiously focuses his eyes on the door as he waits for Ms. Maigret.

It is now 5:46, and she still isn't there.

"Fuck!" he mutters. "Is she coming? Damn."

He's startled as the waitress, Shade, stands over him. "I beg your pardon!"

"Oh! Sorry, Shade," he says in an embarrassed tone. "I was thinking out loud. Just get me a Stranded Amber beer for now. I'm waiting for someone."

A few minutes before six, a tall, elegant, blonde, well-built woman enters the pub. It is Juliana Maigret. She sees him, waves, and walks between the tables toward him. As she approaches, he stands to greet her.

Sorry I'm late, she says.

Don't worry. Pas problem, he replies, and asks her to take off her coat and sit and relax. *What would you like to have?* he asks.

The other patrons in the restaurant look at him strangely, because he's gesturing and speaking, but they see no one with him.

Martini, if possible, she says. *I need a fucking drink.*

He gestures to Shade, who comes over to the table. He asks her for a martini for the young lady. Shade looks confused but obliges his request.

What's this weird scheme you're considering? Juliana asks him. *Have you gone completely mad? How can you bring God before a tribunal?*

Listen, Mrs. Maigret, he says but is soon interrupted.

Call me "Juliana." Monsieur Maigret had enough of me and my work and went back to Paris. I'm left alone now, caring for the two young ones, she says in a confident and matter-of-fact tone.

Oh! I'm sorry to hear that, he says, but again she interrupts him and asks in a strong tone of voice that he leave sentimentality aside. *D'accord,* he agrees.

Let's get to business, she says.

He tells her about his childhood, his suspicions about religion, his child sexual abuse, and the hypocrisy of all religions. He explains that all the world's ailments have arisen because of one entity that entices and induces hatred, killing, corruption, and the many holocausts the world has suffered. This entity is God, and it must be punished, just like any being would be. He shares with her a phrase someone once said innocently, "God is not the answer; he is a cancer."

You and I know God doesn't exist. How will we prosecute a phantom? Juliana interjects. *Are you aware how crazy this sounds?*

Yes, Mrs. Maigret. Sorry. I mean "Juliana." But God does exist through his writings in the holy books. Doesn't he?

Then you want to put religions on trial, she says.
*This is ludicrous. Everyone has the right to be stupid. We
can't prosecute stupid people. If we did, ninety percent of
the world would be imprisoned, and more than ninety-eight
percent of the people in America would be incarcerated.
This is absurd.*

*I just need you to draft the indictment so I can present
the complaint to the International Court of Justice. I'm certain we have a case, Juliana.*

He then explains that the holy books constitute
hate speech and promote violence. He says there
are precedents for convicting individuals on such
charges and cites some of the cases listed in Jeremy
Waldron's book *The Harm in Hate Speech.* In 2009 a
member of the Belgian Parliament was convicted
of distributing leaflets with the slogans "Stand up
against the Islamification of Belgium," "Stop the
sham integration policy," and "Send non-European
job seekers home."

In 2006 protesters were convicted of distributing leaflets to Swedish high school students stating
that homosexuality was a "deviant sexual proclivity,"
had "a morally destructive effect on the substance of

society," and was responsible for the development of HIV and AIDS.

In 2008 a French cartoonist was convicted of publishing a drawing of the attack on the World Trade Center in a Basque newspaper with the caption, "We have all dreamed about it. Hamas did it." The European Court of Human Rights affirmed all three convictions and rejected defenses based on freedom of speech.

In Poland a Catholic magazine was fined $11,000 for inciting "contempt, hostility, and malice" by comparing a woman's abortion to the medical experiments at Auschwitz.

Dutch politician Geert Wilders was temporarily barred from entering Britain and labeled a "threat to public policy, public security, or public health" because he made a movie that called the Quran a "fascist" book and described Islam as a violent religion.

In France Brigitte Bardot was convicted of publishing a letter to the interior minister stating that Muslims were ruining France. Furthermore Canada's human rights tribunal has harassed magazines for making anti-Muslim statements and for republishing the infamous Danish Muhammad cartoons.

Also in Canada, Bill Whatcott was charged with promoting hate after he distributed flyers in Regina and Saskatoon in 2001 and 2002 that condemned gay sex as being immoral. The Saskatchewan Human Rights Tribunal found him guilty in 2005, but that decision was later appealed and overturned in 2010. The tribunal then appealed to the country's top court. However, the court left in place the ban on speech that exposes, or tends to expose, persons or groups to hatred.

The idea here, he explains, is that hate speech, as well as writings that incite hate, are unlawful. The holy books are full of such writings as well as incitements to commit murder. Logically, then, they should be banned, and the writer (God) should be held accountable.

OK, OK, Juliana interrupts. She explains that these are isolated cases and asks how he'll accumulate enough evidence to indict God. She finishes her martini, and he calls Shade over for another one.

This requires some serious drinking, don't you think? Juliana asks playfully.

Yes, sure it does. "Please bring us two cognacs, Shade."

The waitress walks away to fetch his drinks, still not comprehending why he wants two of them.

Wait until I tell Maigret about this. He'll laugh his head off, Juliana tells him.

He looks surprised. *Oh! I thought you said—*

She interrupts him. *Yes, we're separated, but we still talk. We have two children and twenty-five years of friendship. There are no hard feelings at all.*

A long discussion ensues between him and Juliana; he uses all his persuasive skills to convince Juliana that God should be tried; she is finally persuaded as she sees his argument compelling and reasonable. She advises him to be discreet and explains that if his plans are leaked to the media, his life and his wife's life will be in serious danger. She assures him, though, that Maigret understands and that they would benefit from his many years of experience as a chief inspector. He nervously drinks his cognac in one shot; he appears restless and confused. Juliana encourages him and assures him that there's nothing to worry about and that she'll help him write the complaint and brief. She asks him about Sofia and their life together. She asks about his deteriorating health, and they both enter a more intimate and personal conversation.

They finish their meeting and get up to leave. He thanks Juliana and kisses her left cheek. She does the same and assures him she'll be in touch. Then he pays the bill and exits Simzzy's by himself.

He trudges toward home slowly and decides to take a walk along the beach, as he feels he needs to clear his head. He thinks of Juliana driving home, parking her car, and going to her apartment. In his mind he sees her pick up the phone as she's undressing and place a call to Maigret. He hears her tell Maigret about her meeting then ask for his advice. After she realizes Maigret isn't taking her seriously, she hangs up and says, *Va te faire foutre*, which means "Go fuck yourself."

* * *

It is close to 9:30 p.m., and Sofia is quite worried about him and his whereabouts. She picks up the phone and calls his cell. She realizes his phone is off, as the voice mail picks up right away. Soon after she hears the front door open.

"*Amore mio,* is that you?" she calls out. "I was terribly worried about you. Where have you been? Why is your phone off?"

He hears her, but he's in no mood to answer, talk, or argue. He approaches her, kisses her, and throws his tired body onto the sofa. He closes his eyes, and neither he nor Sofia knows for sure whether he is asleep or merely in a daze.

CHAPTER SEVEN:

THE COMPLAINT

It's 3:15 a.m. He is either fully awake or in a delirium state again. He slowly tries to get out of bed without waking up Sofia. In his clumsiness, however, he knocks the side table, and the lamp on top of it falls, crashes, and breaks into pieces on the wooden floor.

Sofia wakes up startled. "*Che cosa è il, amore mio?*"

He quickly answers, "*Niente, niente, Ms. Sofia Di Marco. Tomare a dormire.*"

He asks her to go back to sleep. She sits up in bed and sees him trying picking up the pieces of the broken Tiffany lamp. He tells her he can't sleep and is going to write. She realizes he isn't himself, because he calls her "Ms. Sofia Di Marco." He rarely calls her by her maiden name. When he does, she knows he isn't well.

"Do you want me to be with you?" she asks in a sensual voice.

"No, darling. Go to sleep. I'm sorry I woke you," he coldly replies.

"*A che ora e il, amore mio?*" she softly asks.

"*Dopo tre.*" He tells her it is after three and continues to pick up the broken glass from the floor.

As she lies down, the grief is evident in her eyes. There might even be a drop or two of tears, but he doesn't notice. He leaves the bedroom, goes to his study, turns on the computer, and considers whether he wants a cup of coffee. He decides to make a cup of espresso forte while waiting for the computer to start up.

He brings his coffee to his desk and pulls out the Human Rights Council Complaint Procedure from the many papers on his desk. He takes a glance at it, and a section attracts his attention. It reads, "The complaint procedure addresses consistent patterns of gross and reliably attested violations of all human rights and all fundamental freedoms occurring in any part of the world and under any circumstances.

Please detail, in chronological order, the facts and circumstances of the alleged violations, including dates, places, and alleged perpetrators and how you consider that the facts and circumstances described violate your rights or that of the concerned person(s)."

He jots down his ideas regarding where God has gone wrong in regard to the writings in the holy books—writings that incite hate, crime, murder, mayhem, and evildoing against humanity at large. He starts with the Torah and Old Testament as being the original texts of bloodbath.

He writes:

> *In Leviticus 20:13, it is written, "If a man lies with a man as one lies with a woman, both of them have done what is detestable. They must be put to death; their blood will be on their own heads."*

He underlines "Put to death."

> *When King David orders a census of the people, God gets angry. "And God was displeased with that thing; therefore he smote Israel" (1 Chronicles 21:7); "And the angels of the Lord*

*[destroyed] throughout all the coasts of Israel...
So the Lord sent pestilence upon Israel, and
there fell seventy thousand men" (Chronicles
21:12–14). God orders the killing of humans he
supposedly created and loved. He orders another
attack in Joshua 6:20. "When the trumpets
sounded, the army shouted, and at the sound of
the trumpet, when the men gave a loud shout,
the wall collapsed; so everyone charged straight
in, and they took the city. Joshua 6:21 states,
"They devoted the city to the Lord and destroyed
with the sword every living thing in it—men
and women, young and old, cattle, sheep, and
donkeys."*

*In Judges 21, God orders the murder of all the
people of Jabesh-Gilead, except the virgin girls; he
tells his people to take the virgins and to forcibly
marry them.*

*And in Judges 21:20–21, the Bible says,
"Therefore they instructed the children of
Benjamin, saying, 'Go, lie in wait in the vineyards and watch; and just when the daughters
of Shiloh come out to perform their dances, then*

*come out from the vineyards, and every man
catch a wife for himself."*

*In 2 Kings 10:18–27, God orders the mur-
der of all the worshipers of a different God. "Go
in, kill them; let none come out...And they killed
them with the edge of the sword."*

*In Genesis 16:7–9, God commands the
Egyptian slave Hagar to go back into enslavement
and generate children for her master, though she
does not want to do so, as she says, "I'm running
away from my mistress Sarai."*

*In Genesis 19:5, it states when all the men
of the city surrounded Lot's house and said,
"Where are the men who came to you tonight?
Bring them out to us so that we can have sex with
them." (Genesis 19:5, NIV) By ancient custom,
the visitors were under Lot's protection. Lot was
so infected by the wickedness of Sodom that he
offered the homosexuals his two virgin daughters instead. Furious, the mob rushed up to break
down the door.*

*The angels struck the rioters blind! Leading
Lot, his wife, and two daughters by the hand,*

the angels hurried them out of the city. The girls' fiancés would not listen and stayed behind.

Lot and his family fled to a tiny village called Zoar. The Lord rained down burning sulfur on Sodom and Gomorrah, destroying the buildings, the people, and all the vegetation in the plain.

Lot's wife disobeyed the angels, looked back, and turned into a pillar of salt.

Furthermore, in Genesis 38:10, God murders Onan for refusing to become sexually involved with his sister-in-law.

He researches and writes all of this with a heavy heart. Yet he is determined to bring God to trial and continues to collect evidence.

He moves to the third holy book, the Quran. In his mind there is nothing that is told by God that can or should be taken lightly or unconscientiously.

In Surah 2:190, although God states that he does not like transgressors, he tells his followers to "kill them, [non believers], wherever you overtake them and expel them from wherever they have expelled you."

And to make matters worse and to torment humanity at large and create conflict, prejudice, and hate, God argues that all he has written in the past is void and now "the only true religion in the sight of God is Islam" (Surah 3:19).

In Surah 3:118–119, he continues to promote more prejudice, hate, and even violence by writing, "Believers, do not make friends with any but your own people...They desire nothing but your ruin... You believe in the entire Book...When they meet you they say, 'We, too, are believers.' But when alone, they bite their fingertips with rage."

God clearly incites acts of terrorism when he says, "If you should die or be slain in the cause of God, His forgiveness and His mercy would surely be better than all the riches" (Surah 3:156). Later he says, "Seek out your enemies relentlessly" (Surah 4:104).

God clearly encourages and approves of slavery and bondage when he writes, "Forbidden to you are...married women, except those you own as slaves" (Surah 4:24).

Again we find a clear, intentional incitement of hatred and bigotry—one that is also dreadfully perplexing, to say the least—when God says, "The Jews and Christians say: 'We are the children of God and His loved ones.' Say: why then does He punish you for your sins?" (Surah 5:18).

God adds, "O you who have believed, do not take the Jews and the Christians as allies. They are [in fact] allies of one another. And whoever is an ally to them among you, then indeed, he is [one] of them" (Surah 5:51).

With intent to cause harm and mayhem, God writes, "Make war on them until idolatry shall cease and God's religion shall reign supreme" (Surah 8:39).

He adds, "Make war on the leaders of unbelief...Make war on them: God will chastise them at your hands and humble them. He will grant you victory over them" (Surah 9:12–14). And he further stresses, "Fight against such as those to whom the Scriptures were given [Jews and Christians]...until they pay tribute out of hand and are utterly subdued" (Surah 9:29–30); "If you do not fight, He will punish you sternly and replace you by other men" (Surah 9:38); and "Believers, make war on the infidels who dwell around you. Deal firmly with them" (Surah 9:123).

He has enough now and becomes saddened and stressed, so he takes a rest from writing. He gets up and heads to the kitchen to make another cup of espresso forte. As he rinses his glass, a seizure strikes him, and he falls to the floor, making a loud noise that awakens Sofia. She rushes to the kitchen and lies on the floor, and as she always does when he's in such a state, she holds him tightly while he convulses. She whispers to him, but it seems he isn't in the real realm of life.

Suddenly he awakes from the seizure but is consumed by the complaint. He hears Sofia talking to him, but he can make nothing of what she says. She pulls him up from the floor and gently leads him to bed. She lies to his right and opens her left arm as a gesture to hug him. He rests his head on her breast and feels secure and gratified.

It is now almost 6:30 a.m., and he falls asleep next to Sofia. She ensures he is safe in her arms, and she falls asleep as well.

Just before eight he opens his eyes, stares at the ceiling, and gets a bizarre feeling of not being able to move. He needs to get up, but he can't. He feels as though he's completely paralyzed from head to toe. He explains to Sofia his predicament, but no words come out of his mouth. He thinks he might be dreaming, but he isn't. He's a transient between life and death.

This impasse lasts for fifteen minutes, and then he says, "Good morning, Princess Sofia. How did you sleep, *amore mio?*"

"*Amore, how are you today? Buono matina, amore.*" Sofia's sexy voice breaks the silence in the air and brings a smile to his face.

"*I did a lot of writing, preparing for the complaint to bring God to justice. I'll call Juliana today and see if she's willing to meet with me and discuss the indictment,*" he explains to Sofia, who has no idea what he's talking about, or who this Juliana is.

"Sofia, let me ask you something," he continues. "Do you think there are mafia bosses who actually pulled a trigger to kill someone? Did Hitler personally kill anyone, except his dog, which he poisoned? The answer is likely no. Well, as the same is true for God. Assuming he has killed no one but orders the killing, torture, and mayhem of millions, how different is he from a mafia boss or Hitler? Why do authorities go after mafia bosses if they kill no one?

Why is the word *Hitler* taboo if he himself killed no one? This is certainly bizarre. I must bring that entity to justice."

He continues to natter to Sofia, who is profoundly startled, confused, and somewhat frightened. "Are you sure you want to go through with this, *amore*?" she says in a shaky voice. "I'm worried for your life. There are many crazy people out there, many of whom are religiously zealous. Your life could be in danger, *amore*."

He tells her he will never give up until his last breath. She begs him to be cautious and safe. She stays close to him and tries to comfort him though she is terrified of his thoughts.

CHAPTER EIGHT:

MEETING AT 555

He calls Juliana Maigret and asks if she can meet him at 555 Restaurant on Pine Avenue in Long Beach. She tells him she can, but Monsieur Maigret, who arrived two days ago from Paris, will accompany her, if he doesn't mind. He thinks for a moment and asks whether six-thirty would work with her. She says she'll meet him then.

At 6:12, his taxi arrives at 555 Restaurant, and he pays the fare and exits. He enters the restaurant and tells the hostess about his reservation for three. She asks that he wait for five minutes; she's a bit bemused, as she sees only one person, not three as the reservation shows. Before the five minutes are over, he sees Juliana, beautiful as ever, dressed in a long blue dress; her short, gorgeous hair is curled. She's wearing a pair of expensive-looking shoes, and a pearl necklace adorns her neck. Next to her is a medium-built man who looks very strong. His hair is slightly receding, and he has a Gallic-looking nose that gives him a bourgeois French look. He's neither tall nor short, but a little husky. He wears a hat and holds a cigar on the left side of his lips. He is well groomed and his eyes radiate confidence. He is a typical commissioner or inspector detective.

The pretty hostess takes him to his table; the table is square and sits four people. The restaurant's atmosphere is elegant and pleasant. Although it was full of patrons, both by the bar and at tables, the only sound that can be heard is the voice of the piano man singing romantic slow tunes.

He doesn't feel at ease meeting Maigret, but soon he and Maigret get acquainted and converse about everything from politics to religion to culture to language, but they haven't yet discussed the main topic—the complaint against God.

There are a few moments of silence before Maigret finally says, *Juliana has told me about your new project. It sounds fascinating yet dangerous. Are you abso-lutely certain you want to go through with this?*

Absolutely. I'm determined to bring this entity to justice, he adamantly responds, but with some fear in his heart.

He pulls something from a file in his hand; it's the list of accusations he wrote the night before. He hands it to Juliana.

Here are some of God's atrocities against humanity, he says, and explains that they could also discredit God's writings by showing the many contradictions in all three holy books. He adds that they could bring up the atrocities in Africa, such as the abuse of women and children; they could bring up Mexico's intoler-able corruption; they could dig up more informa-tion on the madness in the Middle East; they could convey China and America's abuse of basic human rights and atrocities from other parts of the world if necessary. He supports his argument by stating that governments go after mafia bosses and the lead-ers of other governments, though these individu-als aren't directly involved in the killing or torture of humanity—even Hitler, who, as far as he knew, never killed a person in his life.

Does that mean Hitler, mafia bosses, and government officials are free of guilt? They certainly are not, he says. *So what do you think, Juliana?*

Let me read this and give it a bit of thought. I'll call you tomorrow, D'accord? she says, which comforts him.

D'accord, bien sûr, he replies. *We need to include the New Testament as well, because Christians argue that things changed after Jesus, but they didn't. The messages in the Book of Revelations are quite significant. They prove that the nature of God hasn't changed just because of the birth of Jesus. God's nature always has been vindictive, abusive, and violent.*

Maigret interjects; *I was talking with some friends at a bar in Montmartre on a hill in the north of Paris, one of whom was Pierre Alexander. Pierre finds the idea intriguing and thinks it is feasible considering how religions influence, if not bring about, current events around the world.*

Do you mean Pierre from Agence France-Presse? Juliana asks.

Maigret replies in the affirmative.

Oh! That could present a serious problem. She explains that Pierre could write something about their plan in the press. She adds that regardless of how insignificant the leak might seem, the media would pick up on it. No one has dared to bring God to justice before. Maigret apologizes, *I am so sorry; I may have underestimated the seriousness of the situation.* He says, *we must be very careful and discreet from here on out.*

They finish their meeting and bid one another farewell.

I'll call you tomorrow, Juliana tells him.

D'accord, mon amie, he replies. He shakes Maigret's hand and departs 555 Restaurant alone.

* * *

"Hello, Sofia, *amore mio.* I'm home. How are you, *mio cuore dolce?*"

He greets his wife but doesn't see her. He hears her from the bedroom.

"*Ciao, amore mio,*" she calls out.

He enters the bedroom and hugs her tightly, as though he is seeking a refuge. She hugs him back and asks if all is well. He tells her about Maigret and what he said regarding Pierre Alexander from Agence France-Press. She turns pale and looks confused and alarmed. She knows neither Juliana nor Maigret, and again she isn't even sure what her husband is talking about. She's just been going along with him, knowing he isn't well.

"*Amore*, this is very dangerous," Sofia says. "You're putting your life in danger. What if this Pierre Alexander writes something about your plan to bring God to justice? Do you know what that means? Our lives will be turned upside down. I told you there are a lot of mad people around us."

"Yes, *amore mio*. I'm aware. Please don't worry," he says in a soothing voice. "This is simply a matter of law and order."

They go to bed, and although they are very tense, they make love passionately. He is exceptionally edgy and certainly needs some relief. After making love, they hug each other and fall asleep.

A short while later, he wakes up suddenly. "*Amore mio*," he says, "I hear some strange sounds. Wake up. Let's go see what's going on."

He shakes Sofia, but she doesn't wake up. He shakes her harder, but she's like a dead body, deeply asleep.

"Please, *mio amore*, wake up."

He pleads with her to no avail. He covers his face with the blanket, moves very close to Sofia, and keeps his eyes wide open and his ears attentive. The strange noise soon stops. It takes him some time to fall back into his normal—that is, irregular -sleep.

The next morning he gets up at six twenty-five. He makes himself an espresso forte and places it on his desk. He opens the front door, picks up his daily paper, and takes it to his desk.

Then he turns on his computer, takes a sip of coffee, and reads the headlines. He turns the paper page by page, and on page four he sees something that attracts his attention. It is neither a major article nor a report that deserves attention. It is a small square on the bottom left of page four with the headline, "California Man Plans to Bring God before the International Court of Justice." With a disconcerted feeling, he continues to read. The story starts by indicating the source—Agence France-Press, Paris. He puts the paper down and screams, "Shit! Shit! Fucking Maigret."

He realizes the seriousness of the matter but tries to comfort himself by attempting to persuade himself that no one will read it.

He decides not to tell Sofia, so as not to alarm her, but before he picks up the phone and calls Juliana, she materializes before him. In a shaky voice, he tells her what he just read. She seems startled and confused and calls upon Maigret, who also emerges. He's wondering what the commotion is about.

We have to be very discreet and cautious. I worked all night on the complaint. I'm sure we have what we need to proceed. Just be careful. Does Sofia know? Juliana asks.

No, no. I can't tell her. She's already panicking and constantly warns me of the danger of such an endeavor.

Shit. Don't tell her anything. Hide the paper. D'accord?

Oui, he says. *I'll do just that.*

We'll talk later and arrange for a meeting in a safer place. She sighs deeply and utters all the expletives she knows in French, English, and even Italian. *Merde! Damn! Cazzo! Fuck! Putain!* she screams.

Don't worry, mon douce amour. I'll take care of any obstacles that may arise, Maigret assures her.

They both leave. Juliana goes to the shower, as though it's her house, and Maigret goes to the ocean for a swim and to clear his head. He's thinking of Salvo Bruno. Salvo Bruno is a brutal detective who works for the Los Angeles Police Department and has strong ties with the FBI. Maigret remembers the days when they worked together solving difficult cases. He gets out of the water, dries himself, and walks into the house, where Juliana is preparing coffee and breakfast. Petit déjeuner *Maigret?*

She asks her husband if he wants breakfast. Maigret tells her he just wants a cup of espresso. Then he asks Juliana if she remembers Salvo Bruno.

How can I forget? she says.

She explains her memories of Salvo Bruno and the danger he and Maigret faced while working together. Maigret tells her he'll call him and explain the situation just in case she and Sofia and her husband encounter serious problems. Juliana encourages the idea and explains that she's determined to do what she was planning to do—help bring God to justice. The whole time, Sofia is in her bedroom asleep and has no idea what's going on with her husband.

Soon after, Maigret gets on the phone with the Los Angeles Police Department and asks for Detective Salvo Bruno.

A few moments later, the detective answers the phone. *This is Salvo. Who's calling?*

You'll never guess who this is, Maigret says.

Son of a bitch! Maigret! Morris Maigret. Holy shit! I'd recognize your voice anywhere. Where you calling from?

I am in Los Angeles, Salvo.

What the fuck are you doing in fucking LA? Salvo anxiously asks.

I came to see Juliana. Do you remember Juliana?

Sure I do, you son of a bitch. How can I forget? I heard she's a hot attorney now. How is she? I haven't seen her since you went back to Paris.

She's very well, Maigret says. *Listen, I need to see you. There's something we need to discuss…OK? Meet me at the Standard on Sunset Boulevard. Do you remember it?*

Of course I do, you asshole. My past is never dead. We used to have a lot of fun there—us and the gang. How about nine o'clock tomorrow night? How does that sound?

Great. I'll see you there, next to the girl in the glass. I miss looking at that sexy girl, Maigret says playfully.

OK. You'll see her tomorrow night. Maybe it'll be your lucky night, and you can take her out of that fucking glass and show her some fun, Salvo says.

You're the same Salvo, always the same. See you at nine o'clock sharp tomorrow night, Maigret tells him and hangs up the phone.

Salvo Bruno is an intelligent detective in his midthirties. He is a tall, well-built man. His sharp eyes are most noticeable; they radiate intelligence, confidence, and critical thinking ability. He keeps his hair very short and at times he wears a hat. He is a heavy smoker and tends to light one cigarette from the butt of another. He is always chewing gum and with that and with a cigarette always between his lips, he tends to speak from the left side of his mouth. Salvo is highly respected among his colleagues at the LAPD.

* * *

When the phone rings, he rushes to pick it up, thinking it's Juliana. It's Monique, Sofia's best friend. After a short chat with her, he calls Sofia to the phone, and she and Monique talk for rather a long time. When she finishes the call, he asks Sofia what the conversation was about.

"You were on the phone for a long time, *amore mio*. Is anything wrong with Monique?" he asks, and waits attentively for an explanation.

She explains that Monique is having problems with her husband, who's from the Middle East. She tells him the husband is getting far too involved with some unscrupulous people at the mosque he attends regularly. She explains that his personality has changed and that he's become violent. The husband doesn't like his wife's clothing or her outings with friends and seems to detest her independence. He talks to her constantly about converting to Islam and avoiding infidels. Even his appearance has changed; he now has a long beard, wears a white dress that falls just below his knees, and wears slippers instead of shoes. He also has bought a white hat that he wears all the time, and he constantly prays or recites verses from the Quran. Sofia tells him she's worried about Monique and her safety.

She confides in him that her friend met a handsome young man who lives in Century City close to her office and started up an affair with him.

"If her husband discovers that, he'll kill her for sure. I'm so worried about her," Sofia explains in a gloomy voice.

He takes all this in and interprets it according to how his ill mind works and how progressed his paranoia has become.

"Did you tell Monique anything about my plan to bring God to justice?" he asks Sofia in a panicky voice.

"Actually, yes. Last time we were out, I mentioned it but didn't give any details."

"Shit! This is serious," he says. "Emotional people like many Middle Easterners and many fanatic Christians in America are far too zealous and could certainly cause a great deal of harm."

"I'm meeting her today for lunch," Sofia tells him. "I'll ask her not to mention any of this to her husband. I hope she hasn't said anything already."

Sofia explains that Monique was a pretty, young girl, about twenty-two years old, when she met her husband while studying political science in Barcelona. Monique is slim, and of medium height, with a petite build. Her eyes are big, brown, and sparkling with life, and her small body makes her very attractive and desirable. Her smile resembles the subtle look on the lips of Johannes Vermeer's *The Girl with the Pearl Earring*. She looks mysterious and quite intelligent. The boy was a simple waiter in a local restaurant. He was charming and persuaded Monique to marry him. Once she finished her degree, they got married and came to California. They had a wonderful first three months together, and then everything went downhill from there. They have been married for three years now. She met her lover, Alex, during her first year of marriage, and they've been seeing each other since. Her strange husband repeatedly hits her and treats her as if she's his servant, but she's too embarrassed to report him to the police or tell anyone about it. She hasn't mentioned any of this to her close friends, except Sofia.

Feeling very stressed, he calls Juliana to tell her this story. He gives Sofia's girlfriend the pseudonym of "Marina" and her husband the name "Morsi." Juliana expresses discomfort with the news and with the fact that the French press mentioned their plan to try God. She, too, is very stressed, but she says they'll go ahead with the complaint and tells him she's finishing the brief.

There's an enormous amount of evidence for us to convict God on many charges, she tells him. *We'll add pictures of the atrocities in Syria, Lebanon, Afghanistan, Pakistan, India, Africa, and even the United States. We have a very strong case. I'm working on this day and night,* she assures him. *We'll get it to the court before long.*

CHAPTER NINE:

MAIGRET MEETS SALVO

I t's Wednesday. He's in his room trying to read, write, or do anything. Instead he's just in deep thought. Suddenly, around 8:15 p.m., he leaves the house and drives away. Sofia has no idea where he's going.

Around 9:00 p.m. Salvo leaves his Lexus sports car with the valet and walks into the Standard. Both he and Maigret are anxious to see each other after so long. From a distance he sees Maigret and rushes to greet him.

My friend, it's been a long time, he tells Maigret. *You haven't changed a bit—you're the same ol' Maigret I've always known."*

You've always been a sweet-talker, you son of a bitch. Of course the years have left their marks on my face and body, but you haven't aged a bit, Maigret tells Salvo.

They both finish their small talk and find a quiet corner in the bar. They sit down, and immediately a pretty waitress in a short skirt and a revealing top places napkins on the table and asks him what he would like to drink. Salvo and Morris look at each other and say at the same time, *Cognac.* Just like the old days.

He orders three glasses of cognac and asks that his glass be placed and tilted above another glass filled with warm water; he likes his cognac warm. The pretty waitress, named Jasmine, walks away with the order, wondering why he's ordering three drinks, as he's alone.

How is Mattie, Salvo? Maigret inquires. *I miss her and think of both of you often.*

He is quickly interrupted by Salvo, who says in a gloomy voice, *Mattie left me four and half years ago. She couldn't handle my demanding work and felt lonely. We're still friends, and we talk sometimes.*

I'm sorry, Salvo. That's the business we're in. What can we do? That's what happened between Juliana and me. We're friends and talk often too. In fact I'm staying with her now. I enjoy being with the two young ones. I can't tell you how much I miss them.

As they drink their cognac, they talk about Juliana's project, the leaking of information to the French press, and what may come out of it. Maigret expresses his fears that Marina (aka "Monique"), Sofia's best friend, is married to a fanatic named Morsi. Maigret also tells Salvo that Marina has been having an affair with a man who lives in Century City.

Wait a minute, Morris, Salvo interrupts. *So what we have here is a cracked man who wants to prosecute God in the International Court of Justice. This man is a friend of Juliana, and she's helping him with the complaint. Then we have, Sofia's, this guy's wife's friend, who's married to a nut and is having an affair. And to top that off, we have the French press publishing an article about the plan to indict God. Now that is a fucked-up situation that nothing good can come out of.*

I know. I know, Salvo. This is a tricky situation. Juliana is supporting this eccentric friend with his indictment, and she won't listen to reason. That's why I'm here. I'm concerned.

You should be concerned, my friend, Salvo says. *This is really a fucked-up condition. It reminds me of the case you and I worked on—that mafioso named Fatzio, I think. No, his name was Marconi. You remember Marconi?*

How can I forget? You were shot and almost died. Of course I remember. Damn! Time really passes quickly. That was eighteen years ago or so, right? Maigret asks.

I think it was twenty-one years ago, says Salvo.

They continue talking over more cognac until past midnight. They say they'll keep each other informed and keep an eye on the situation.

It was great seeing you, Maigret, Salvo says.

You too, Maigret tells him. *Just like old times.*

* * *

Maigret returns to Juliana's apartment. He rings the bell, and she comes to the door asking, *Who's there?*

It's me, Morris, he says.

Juliana cautiously opens the door, sees him, and releases the chain. Maigret enters, takes off his jacket, and recites what has just taken place during his meeting with Salvo. He assures Juliana again that Salvo Bruno will help them if necessary.

Their conversation is interrupted by the ringing of Juliana's cell phone. She responds and hears a distraught voice on the other end. It's Sofia Di Marco's husband.

Hi, Juliana. It's me. Have you seen Sofia? She isn't home, and I'm terrified. I heard some noise; some strange people were here—two men. A little while after I came home from the Standard, I went and opened the door and saw them running off. I was petrified. The words "blasfemous basterds" are spray-painted in red on my front door. He continues in a trembling voice, *"I'm really scared, Juliana. Please find my wife and ask her to come home quickly; it's after midnight, and I'm really frightened.*

He begins to cry uncontrollably. Juliana tries to comfort him and tells him that she and Maigret are on their way to his apartment. It's now forty-five minutes after midnight. Maigret decides to call Salvo so that they might be able to get some fingerprints. Maigret picks up his cell phone and dials Salvo's number. He's very disappointed when his voice mail picks up.

Salvo, this is Maigret, he says. *Something has come up, and we need your help. Please, if you get this message, meet Juliana and me at 30001 Bay Shore in Long Beach.*

As Juliana parks her car along the curb in front of his apartment, she sees Salvo in his Lexus parking behind her.

Hey, Salvo! Long time, she says.

After the initial greetings, the three of them—Juliana, Maigret, and Salvo—come to the door and knock. He makes sure who's at the door then opens it slowly. Then he cries and shows extraordinary worry. He hasn't heard from Sofia since he left for the Standard, and her mobile phone has been off; now there's that phrase on the door.

Salvo calls the police department and asks for forensics to come to the apartment to check for prints and the materials used in the vandalism. He gives them the address and asks that the case be considered a hate crime with the intent of intimidation. Before long, police cars, marked and unmarked, are surrounding the apartment building.

Salvo asks him if he heard or saw anything but gets no concrete answers. The detective then looks around the front door in an attempt to decipher the mystery at hand. He takes a report, collects pictures of the crime scene, and assures him they'll get to the bottom of this.

Then he dials a number.

"Hello?" Sofia says.

"Hey! Where are you, *amore mio*? I'm worried sick about you. Why was your phone off? Come home right away. I'm here with Maigret and Salvo. Something terrible happened."

"Yes, everything is OK, and I'm OK. Just come home now. All right?"

Sofia is bewildered by the call. She doesn't understand much of what her husband says. She's been in the apartment, in their bedroom, the whole time.

A short while later, Sofia enters the living room and, startled and confused, approaches her husband. He hugs her and tells her what has just happened. Sofia explains that she's been in the bedroom the entire time. She can't explain why her cell phone was turned off but now it's on again. He isn't grasping what she says. She doesn't see any kind of vandalism of the front door.

He's severely worried about what happened and wonders whether Marina's husband, Morsi, had anything to do with it. Seriously concerned and confused, Sofia goes back to bed.

Salvo Bruno approaches him and asks if he has any idea who might have done something like this. He tells Salvo about Marina and her husband, Morsi. He also tells him that he read in the local newspaper a short piece about his plans to bring God to the International Court of Justice. So at this point it could be anyone.

But how could they know where I live? he asks Salvo.

Interesting question, he replies.

Outside the apartment building, Maigret walks around, looking for clues. Not far from the door, he finds something that attracts his attention—a piece of paper on which "30001 Bay Shore" is written. Also written are words "blasfemous basterds." He hands the note to Salvo and asks that he send it to forensics for analysis. Salvo takes the paper with a rubber-gloved hand and places it in a plastic evidence bag.

Salvo suggests that Sofia and her husband stay with Juliana and Maigret for a while until they clear up this situation.

Sofia's husband thinks she will never agree to leave their apartment, so he takes his car and follows Maigret and Juliana. They drive slowly through a crowd of curious neighbors who want to know what is happening and why there are so many police cars around the apartment building. Salvo and some forensic-team members stay behind in the apartment, looking for more clues.

CHAPTER TEN:

FORENSICS

At the forensic lab of the Los Angeles Police Department, a team of experts is looking at the fingerprints they collected, but the only prints they can find belong to the residents and their friends. The expert working on the piece of paper Maigret found is trying to identify the type and source of the paper.

She finds various fingerprints on the paper. After forensic examination of the type of paper, she discovers a motel's name impeded within the texture of the paper itself and cannot possibly be seen by a naked eye. She, then, determines that the paper is originally from a motel in Anaheim. She also determines that the writings are not fresh; she thinks the message was written at least twenty hours before midnight on Wednesday, June third. She calls Salvo Bruno and shares her findings. He takes the name of the motel and writes it on a slip of paper and places it in his jacket pocket. He asks that she send the fingerprints to the lab for analysis.

It is now Thursday, June fourth, around about midday. Salvo gets up and walks toward his car. While walking, he picks up his cell phone and calls Morris Maigret.

Hi, Morris, he says. *I have some news. I'm on my way to Anaheim. I'll pick you up on the way.*

Maigret wonders what the news could be. He's unable to reach Juliana; he thinks she may be in court. He anxiously awaits Salvo, and before long, Salvo's Lexus pulls in front of Juliana's apartment building. Salvo waves his hands from the car as he sees Maigret at the window. Maigret picks up his jacket and goes to the car, opens the passenger door, and throws his heavy body in the seat. He greets Salvo while fastening his seatbelt.

What's the news, Salvo? he impatiently asks.

Salvo tells him about the forensic department's findings and says he's going to the motel where the piece of paper came from. They also have some fin-gerprints, which they've sent to the lab to for analysis.

Maigret interjects, *I'm curious why the misspelled phrase "blasfemous basterds" appears under the address. Is it possible that the individuals who vandalized the door don't know how to spell in English or that English is their second language?*

That's brilliant, Maigret. You haven't lost it, old boy. Unquestionably this makes sense, Salvo says, and thinks for a moment. *Didn't you mention that Sofia's friend, Marina, is married to a fanatic nut? I forgot his fucking name. Mustafa or Mubarak or something like that.*

Morsi, Maigret says in a very calm voice that is hard to decipher.

What? Salvo questions.

Maigret explains to Salvo that yes, indeed, Marina is married to an abusive fanatic whose name is Morsi. *He attends a mosque in Anaheim actually*, he says. *I need to confirm with Sofia's husband whether Marina knows anything about the project to impeach God and if she said anything to that asshole.* Maigret picks up his cell phone and dials the number for Juliana's house, but no one answers. He leaves a message, ask-ing that Sofia's husband call him right away.

Within five minutes Maigret's phone rings.

Morris Maigret. Ah! Thank you for calling me back. First how are you? I'm sorry I left without saying good-bye; I didn't want to disturb you. By the way, did your wife ever speak with her friend Marina about the project you and Juliana are pursuing? Oh, mon dieu! Oh, merde! Do you think she said anything to her nut husband, Morsi? I see... you aren't sure. D'accord. I'll see you later. Take good care of yourself. Cursing, Maigret hangs up the phone and tells Salvo that most likely Morsi knows about the plan to file a complaint against God.

* * *

Sofia's husband is still at Juliana's apartment. He misses Sofia. He is too close to his wife, like a child who seeks his mother's protection. Again he is in one of those phantasmagoric states. He talks but makes no sense; he mumbles incomprehensible words.

Sofia is alarmed, as she doesn't know where her husband is. She calls for him, but he doesn't answer. When she calls his cell phone, he answers and speaks about events and places that Sofia has no idea about. For the first time, she questions whether

her husband suffers from a serious mental illness; he has been talking to himself a lot, and his moods change often and suddenly. He also talks with and about people she neither sees nor knows about.

As soon as he returns home, she hugs him tightly and suggests that he sees a doctor. She tries to be very careful with her choice of words and sensitive to his feelings, as his demeanor may change in a matter of seconds, even though he has never been violent with her in the past. He is always calm but deep in thought. Lately, however, he has been rather withdrawn and seems to avoid his friends whenever they ask him to get together with them. He also has lost interest in grooming himself and has become rather sloppy in his attire.

He isn't responsive to her and doesn't react to her suggestion to see a doctor. He's in his own world, and his world seems to be as far from the sphere of reality as scientifically possible.

Salvo and Maigret arrive at the motel in Anaheim. Salvo parks his Lexus in the lot, and they both enter the office. Salvo politely introduces himself to the desk clerk as an LAPD detective and says he has some questions. The clerk, who is about thirty-five-years-old bald and untidy man in a rather old blue jacket with the name Ali Mahmoud tag on it, and is of Jordanian origin and speaks English in a broken accent; he also manages the cheap unclean fifteen--room motel in Anaheim, responds in a confused voice, asking why an LAPD officer would be working in Orange County. Salvo assures the clerk that he just has a few questions and that it's nothing serious. While Salvo is talking with the clerk, Maigret looks around and picks up a small notepad with the motel's logo; he also picks up a box of matches and puts the notepad and matches in his pocket.

Salvo asks the clerk about the guests who registered at the motel between May thirty-first and June fourth. The clerk shows him the registration book. Salvo sees four foreign-sounding names and writes down their contact information. He asks the clerk whether any of the guests behaved in an unusual manner. The clerk asks him for clarification.

Did any of them appear nervous, restless, or up to something? Salvo asks.

The clerk replies in the negative. Salvo asks whether any of the guests arrived at the motel after midnight on Wednesday, June third. The clerk says he worked that whole night and can't remember any-one arriving that late.

Salvo thanks him and tells Maigret, *We're done here, Morris.*

They both walk out of the motel more puzzled than when they arrived.

Salvo informs Maigret that he took down the information for four guests on whom he will run a check at the station. Maigret tells Salvo that he took one the motel's notepads and a box of matches; he removes them from his pocket and hands them to the detective. Salvo places them in his pocket, and they both drive off.

CHAPTER ELEVEN:

THE BRIEF

Juliana has almost completed writing the complaint and brief to indict God. She has identified the parties and counsel for the people. She also has identified and listed an index of authorities, statutes, and rules. She's drafted a strong convincing statement of the case with issues presented as well as a statement of facts, all with clear citations.

She finishes writing the summary of the argument, then the argument itself, along with concrete references to black-letter law and various cases. She's now finishing writing the certification of service. She's very eager to pursue this case.

His phone rings, and he picks it up, though he isn't in a stable state. *Hello. Who's calling?* He forces the words out of his mouth.

Congratulations, friend. The first stage is complete. I stayed up all night writing the brief. It's done and ready to go, Juliana says jubilantly and triumphantly.

That's wonderful, Juliana. Thank you, he says and hangs up.

Juliana wonders what's wrong with him. He doesn't seem himself; she persuades herself that he's hardly himself anyway and goes to bed. In bed she and Maigret talk about their day and everything that's taken place over the past twenty-four hours.

Maigret tells her about his visit with Salvo to the motel in Anaheim and how they found it based on the information from forensics. Juliana tells him she's finished the brief. They discuss the strong possibility that Marina's husband, Morsi, was involved in defacing the door. They agree that it's the only logical conclusion. Exhausted, they both fall asleep.

* * *

While Maigret and Juliana are asleep, Salvo is at the station, working hard to identify the four foreign guests at the motel. None of them seems to be a likely suspect; one person, however, by the name of

Gamal Nour-Eldeen is a resident of Anaheim. Salvo wonders why a resident of Anaheim would stay at a motel only two miles from his home. He theorizes that since Nour-Eldeen is a married man with children, he may be having an affair and rented the motel room for that purpose.

Salvo checks Nour-Eldeen's FBI profile but finds nothing peculiar. Then he checks Morsi's profile, but he doesn't have the man's full name and address; he only knows that he lives in Los Angeles County. It's too late to call Maigret for Morsi's last name and address, so he decides to wait until the next morning to ask for his information. However, he does call the Anaheim Police Department and asks to speak with Detective Raul Del Rio. The detective isn't available, so Salvo leaves a message and asks him to call him back in the morning.

* * *

It's 3:08 a.m. Sofia is awoken by her husband's clumsiness as he's getting up.

Dove si sta andando il, amore mio? she asks where he is going.

I can't sleep, amore mio. I'm going to my desk. Sorry to have woken you. Please go back to sleep, he calmly replies.

He makes his espresso forte and sits at his desk, where he obsessively reviews his notes. For the first time in his life, he realizes that he talks to himself, but this realization doesn't seem to trouble him. What overwhelms him is that he finds that he replies to himself. Yes, he has felt his mother's presence by his bed before and even conducted a conversation with her, but this time is different.

He's at his desk, drinking his coffee, and sees Juliana sitting on the couch in a short skirt with her legs crossed. He even asks her if she wants a cup of espresso. He is certain he isn't alone.

Why are you here at three thirty in the morning, Juliana? he asks her. *Have you had an argument with Maigret?* He receives no reply. *Did Sofia open the door for you?* He asks his third question, waiting to hear answers. Juliana looks at him with a beautiful smile on her face that makes her full lips appear luscious and certainly kissable.

He is precipitously returned to the real world, if there is such a thing as an existent world. He focuses now, realizing that he's entirely alone and that Juliana's presence was a fabrication of his imagination. He shuffles through his documents, studies what he has written for Juliana to include in her brief, and wonders whether he should add anything that might be valuable.

He realizes that his focus has been on part of the Torah and Old Testament in addition to some proof from the Quran. He's now thinking about the time of Jesus, the son of God and the savior. He researches his books and Internet sites to collect viable information.

In the Book of Mathew alone, he finds more than thirty disconcerting and ominous verses. He picks up his writing pad and writes down some of what he finds while searching the New Testament online. He's read this book many times in three different languages. He writes:

"God will come when people least expect him, and then he'll cut them asunder. And there shall be weeping and gnashing of teeth" (Matthew 24:50–5).

Jesus tells us what he has planned for those that he dislikes. They will be cast into an everlasting fire (Matthew 25:4).

"Then shall he say also unto them on the left hand, depart from me, ye cursed into everlasting fire, prepared for the devil and his angels" (Matthew 25:41).

From the book of Mark, he writes:

Jesus says the damned will be tormented forever (Mark 25:46).

Jesus says that those that believe and are baptized will be saved, while those who don't will be damned (Mark 16:16).

Jesus criticizes the Jews for not killing their disobedient children as required by Old Testament law. He also says to them, "You completely invalidate God's command in order to maintain your tradition! For Moses said: Honor your father and your mother; and whoever speaks evil of father or mother must be put to death" (Mark 7:9–10).

From the book of Luke, he cites:

Jesus says that entire cities will be violently destroyed and the inhabitants, thrust down to hell for not receiving his disciples (Luke, 10:10-15).

Jesus says that we should fear God, since he has the power to kill us and then torture us forever in hell (Luke, 12:5).

"Except ye repent, ye shall all likewise perish" (Luke, 13:3–5).

Jesus also believes the story about Sodom's destruction. He says, "Even thus shall it be in the day the Son of man is revealed…Remember Lot's wife" (Luke, 17:29–32).

And from the book of Peter he notes:

"Turning the cities of Sodom and Gomorrah into ashes" (Peter 2:6).

"God will set the entire earth on fire so that he can burn nonbelievers to death" (Peter 3:7).

"When Jesus returns, he'll burn up the whole earth and everything on it" (Peter 3:10).

After two hours, he's dreadfully drained, having read and written down so many ruthless phrases and ominous images. Even so, he's stauncher than ever in his mission. It's now 5:20 a.m., and he's unreservedly confident that God will not only be tried before the International Court of Justice but also convicted.

"The evidence is overwhelming," he says loudly. No court could refuse to address such atrocities, and most judges and juries certainly would convict such an egocentric maniac.

He's in a euphoric state of mind, and endorphins are flooding his fatigued body. It's close to 6:00 a.m., and he hasn't had a minute of sleep all night.

He's tempted to call Juliana and share what he's found with her, but he realizes it's too early and knows she has a court hearing this morning. He decides to wait until late afternoon. His severe paranoia prevents him from communicating with Juliana via e-mail, especially after what happened at his apartment last night. He also keeps in mind the illegal invasion of privacy by the United States government, as bravely revealed by Edward Snowden.

He contemplates going to bed, but he's concerned he'll wake Sofia again, which makes him feel guilty. In fact he often feels guilty toward Sofia. She drives him to his doctor's appointments; she tends to his medical and personal needs; she suffers with him while he suffers from seizures and strange attacks. In addition to all that, his insomnia and restless sleep disturbs her. He doesn't know how to manage his guilt. He decides to go to bed anyway. He needs some energy for what is to come.

CHAPTER TWELVE:

INVESTIGATION

It's Friday, June fifth, early morning at the Los Angeles Police Department. Salvo Bruno arrives at his office, takes off his jacket, and hangs it up. He sits at his desk and reads the messages that were left for him. He notices that Detective Raul Del Rio called him. He looks at his watch, picks up his phone, and calls the Anaheim Police Department. He asks for Detective Del Rio and is immediately connected.

Hello, Raul. How's it going, my friend? Salvo says. *I'm sure you're busy as hell, just like we are here.*

Hey, Salvo! How have you been? I haven't seen or talked to you for a while. What can I do for you?

Salvo explains the situation regarding the vandalism in Long Beach and asks Raul to interview

a man named Gamal Nour-Eldeen. He spells the
name for him and provides him with the address.
He tells him to be discreet because the man is married, and the fact that he spent the night at a motel
two miles away from his house may indicate that he's
having an affair. Raul assures Salvo that he'll contact
him in the afternoon. They share a bit of small talk
and say their good-byes.

Salvo phones Maigret to ask for Morsi's last name
and home address. Maigret says he'll call him back
once he gets the information from Juliana. Salvo
asks whether Maigret would like to go with him to
interview Morsi, and Maigret agrees. Salvo tells him
he'll leave in a few minutes to pick him up.

A short time later, Salvo gets into his car to pick
up Maigret in Long Beach. The traffic on Interstate
5 is terrible, and the heat is unbearable. Although
Salvo has the top of his Lexus down, he really feels
the heat because he isn't driving more than ten miles
an hour. He curses and curses. It takes him an hour
and a half to get from Los Angeles to Long Beach.
By the time he arrives, he's seriously ill tempered.

Just before approaching Juliana's apartment
building, Salvo calls Maigret to say he'll be there in

three minutes. Maigret grabs his jacket and waits at the curb for Salvo. When Salvo arrives, Maigret gets into the car and realizes how cross his friend is.

Fucking freeways shouldn't be called freeways, Salvo says. *No freeway is free anymore; they have to come up with a more appropriate name.*

Oui, mon ami. That's surely true, even in Paris. And it all seems to have happened suddenly, Maigret replies.

They approach Morsi's address, which Maigret got from Juliana. It's an old apartment building in downtown Long Beach. Salvo parks the car, and they get out and go to the third floor to find apartment 309. Salvo knocks on the door and identifies himself as a police detective. After a few knocks, a very pretty, petite woman opens the door. Salvo introduces himself as Detective Bruno and identifies Maigret as his partner. The woman is startled and visibly shaking.

Are you Mrs. Marina Sheikh Ahmad? Salvo asks.

Yes, I am. What happened? Marina replies in a quivering voice. She buttons her open blouse fretfully.

Is your husband home? We need to ask him some questions, Salvo politely says then asks if they can enter the apartment.

Yes, he is. He's in the bedroom praying right now. What's this about? she asks nervously, as she escorts them into the apartment.

Salvo tries to calm her a little. *Nothing to worry about, ma'am. We just want to ask him a few questions.*

A short, dark-skinned man appears from another room. He has black hair, most of which is covered by a round white hat, and he has a long, black, untidy beard. He's wearing a long white dress that stops just before his ankles, and he's barefoot.

Al-salamu alaykum. Good afternoon. I am Morsi. How may I help you? the man says.

Can we all sit down please? Salvo asks.

Sure. Please, please, come sit, Morsi says in a warm, welcoming voice. *Anything to drink? Shall we make tea?*

Salvo and Maigret notice Morsi's accent but see him as courteous and polite. They refuse the offer of tea.

They all sit down at the dining-room table, except Maigret, whose talent for observation makes him notice three newspapers on the kitchen table. He discreetly moves the papers and notices that all of them are opened to pages where headlines about Juliana's project to indict God appear in bold and are circled in red ink. He observes closely. One reads, "California Man Plans to Sue God." The second reads, "God on Trial?" The third states, "God May Appear before a Tribunal." Maigret takes this evidence seriously. He continues to walk around the apartment confidently and quietly.

Salvo begins to question Morsi. *Mr. Sheikh Ahmad, where were you during the evening of Wednesday, June third, and the early morning of Thursday, June fourth?*

I was here, home with my wife, Marina. Why do you ask? he confidently responds.

Both Salvo and Maigret notice Marina's eyes go wide, which makes them doubt Morsi's answer.

So you didn't go out at all, not even to the store or the mosque? Salvo asks, his eyes focused on Marina's facial expressions.

No, not at all. We had dinner. Then I prayed, and we went to bed, Morsi answers again with confidence. The same surprised and frightened look remains on Marina's face. Her entire demeanor changes with Morsi's answers.

Maigret asks if he can talk to Salvo in the kitchen for a minute. Morsi and Maria nod in approval, and Salvo excuses himself.

Maigret points to the three newspapers on the kitchen table. Both Salvo and Maigret hear soft voices from the other room; the voices indicate to them that Marina is arguing with her husband. They leave the kitchen and sit down across from Morsi and Marina at the dining-room table.

Which mosque do you regularly attend, Mr. Sheikh Ahmad? Salvo asks.

Morsi tells him that he goes to several mosques, but the one he goes to the most is near their apartment building.

Do you write English well, Mr. Sheikh Ahmad? Salvo asks, while writing something down on his notepad.

Not really. I speak a little, but I can't read or write English. I'm fluent in Arabic, though. I can read and write very well in Arabic, Morsi replies in a quiet, shameful voice.

Salvo thanks them both and says if he needs any more information, he'll be in touch. As Salvo and Maigret leave the apartment, they exchange glances, as though they've read each other's minds.

As they get into the car, Salvo says, *That son of a bitch is lying through his teeth. He wasn't home that night. Did you see the apprehension on Marina's face and the fear in her eyes?*

Maigret replies in the affirmative and says he believes Morsi is the perpetrator or someone he knows is. He's clearly lying. *Then we saw those newspapers with the headlines circled in red,* he says.

Salvo interrupts, saying that Morsi probably knows where Sofia and her husband live because Sofia is Marina's best friend. But the reality is that Sofia doesn't know anyone named Marina. Her best friend is Monique.

The three them—he, Salvo, and Maigret—arrive at Juliana's apartment. Salvo comes inside with them; Maigret now has a key to Juliana's place, and they sit down in the living room for a drink. It's been a long, tiring day for the three of them.

After some trivial chatting, Salvo says, *So what are your thoughts on this, Maigret? Do you think it was Morsi? It sure appears that way, doesn't it?*

Maigret thinks for a moment then replies. *You must speak with Marina alone. She was unmistakably frightened and shocked by what Morsi said.* Salvo agrees.

Sofia's husband asks if Maigret and Salvo have any more information about the crime. Salvo tells him they believe Marina's husband is involved. He asks him for Marina's personal cell phone number.

He down writes the number on a slip of paper and hands it to Salvo.

Maigret, let's recap here, Salvo says. *We have the newspapers and the circled headlines. We have Morsi being dishonest, and we have Marina appearing frightened and surprised. This appears to be solved.*

Yes, but talk with Marina. I'm sure she'll tell you more, Maigret replies.

Salvo finishes his soft drink quickly and gets up to leave for the office. He says his good-byes, and Maigret says he'll call him in a couple of hours.

* * *

Salvo arrives at his office and immediately calls Marina, who answers the phone.

Mrs. Sheikh Ahmad, this is Detective Salvo Bruno. I'm calling to ask if there's anything you want to tell me. When I visited you this afternoon, I noticed you were somewhat anxious and wanted to say something, but you seemed concerned about your husband. I want you to know that you can talk to me confidentially and off the record.

Marina is quiet for a while then suddenly starts sobbing, and in a somewhat incoherent manner, between tears and words, she says, *Morsi was lying about having been here with me that night. He disappeared for two days and never told me where he was.* She continues to weep.

Please calm down, Mrs. Sheikh Ahmad. Everything is OK and will be OK. Thank you for the information. I promise to keep it off the record, Salvo assures her. He continues, *One last question—do you know why the newspapers on the kitchen table have red circles around specific headlines?*

She replies, *No, I don't, but I know it was Morsi who did that. I saw him doing it and saying things in Arabic I couldn't understand.*

Salvo thanks her again for the information, says good-bye, and hangs up.

He calls his assistants into his office and ask that they place Morsi under surveillance and report all his movements, whereabouts, and contacts to him personally. A short while later, he manages to get the district attorney's office to request a court order to tap Morsi's phone and also to bug his apartment.

Just before 7:00 p.m., Salvo receives a call from Maigret. He explains to Maigret that their initial hunch was simply perfect. He recaps his conversation with Marina and states that Morsi is indeed lying. He informs him that Morsi is now under surveillance and explains that his friend Detective Raul Del Rio is working on Gamal Nour-Eldeen.

* * *

The next morning Raul Del Rio of the Anaheim Police Department calls Salvo at the office and tells him what his investigations of Gamal Nour-Eldeen have revealed.

Good morning, Salvo. I hope it isn't too early for you. Listen, this guy Nour-Eldeen has a long list of records with us that goes back seven years. He was convicted on vandalism charges and convicted for possessing and distributing literature that incites criminal activities and hate. And listen to this—he was convicted and imprisoned for three years on child sexual abuse charges. Guess who the victim was? His little sister, a nine-year-old girl. Can you believe this fucking shit? He's a regular at the local Anaheim mosque and has many friends there. What's the name of the guy in Long Beach? Is it Marsi or something?

Salvo is listening attentively and taking notes. *Morsi is the name. Morsi Sheikh Ahmad,* he replies.

Yeah, that's it. Nour-Eldeen is a friend of this Morsi guy, and they hang out at cafés in Anaheim. We'll place him under surveillance. I'll keep you posted, Salvo. Bye for now.

Thanks, Raul. We'll be in touch. By the way, we also placed Morsi under surveillance. Thanks again.

Salvo hangs up the phone and sinks into deep thoughts. *Fucking contemptible bastards*, he hears himself say.

The forensics department calls Salvo to tell him that the slip of paper Maigret found outside the apartment building has no legitimate fingerprints on it. But they found that the paper itself is a perfect match to the notepad Maigret took from the motel. Salvo is now certain of Morsi's guilt, but he doesn't know whether he acted alone or is a member of a group of possible terrorists. He must patiently wait for more information from the surveillance of Morsi.

The first report Salvo receives is quite disturbing. It's a recorded telephone conversation between Morsi and a man named Ali Almokhtar. The content of the conversation reveals that Morsi is a member of a local terrorist group that plans to attack Disneyland using a thirteen-year-old boy they refer to as the "chosen one," but in this initial recording, there's no specific information about the plan or who Ali Almokhtar or the "chosen one" are.

Nervous and disturbed, Salvo calls his friend Dorothy Lawton at the FBI and explains the entire situation. Dorothy tells Salvo that the case is now in the FBI's hands and that they'll take it from there. Salvo isn't happy with Dorothy's comment but asks that she keep him posted. The conversation ends there, leaving Salvo more than just a little upset.

Salvo calls Maigret and explains,

The fucking FBI wants us off the case. I have just spoken with agent Dorothy and she said that the case in the hands of the FBI now.

Maigret is unhappy but assures Salvo that they'll stay on top of the matter, regardless of the FBI's involvement.

Listen salvo, we have come this far, we are not letting this go; we will have to be on top of any development. Maigret stresses angrily.

CHAPTER THIRTEEN:

THE PSYCHIATRIST

He is in an unusual state. He keeps talking to himself and responding as though he were talking with someone. He's agitated, twitchy, and incomprehensible. He talks of terrorists attacking Disneyland and mentions names Sofia knows nothing about. Quite frightened, she calls his regular doctor, Dr. Robert Shen, who advises her to take him immediately to Long Beach Memorial Hospital.

Although she's frantic, she calmly persuades him to get into her car and drives him a short distance to the hospital.

"Where are we? Where are we going, Sofia?" he asks fretfully.

She tells him they're going to get some serious help. She arrives at the hospital and parks the car.

"Are you OK, honey? Why are we at the hospital?" he asks her firmly. "Did something happen to you, *amore mio?* What's wrong, *amore mio?* You can tell me."

She doesn't reply. She exits the car and leads him by the hand to the hospital entrance. Once inside, she approaches the emergency-room desk.

"Hello. Dr. Shen asked that I bring my husband here right away. He's hallucinating and talking to and answering himself. I think he needs a psychiatric evaluation. Please hurry. I'm not sure I can keep him here with me for long."

A few moments later, the receptionist calls for Sofia. She tells her that they received an urgent message from Dr. Shen and that it will take a moment until a nurse can come out to take her husband in for an evaluation. Several minutes later a nurse appears and asks that they follow her. She takes them both to the hospital's triage area.

She asks Sofia a few questions while taking her husband's vital signs. He seems to be in a twilight zone, unaware of anything that's taking place; Sofia explains to the nurse that he hasn't been himself lately. He's been talking to and answering himself, as though someone were with him. She explains his mood changes and his obsession with the idea of accusing God of human rights violations and prosecuting him. "He constantly talks with a female lawyer named Juliana and her French husband—or boyfriend, I'm not sure. I think his name is Morris Maigret," she says. "I've never seen these people. He seems to be hallucinating."

"Thank you for the information," the nurse tells her. "I'll take him in as soon as a bed is ready."

The nurse sees that he's highly agitated and not in a safe condition. A few minutes later, she takes him to a room, and Sofia follows.

As he lies on a hospital bed in the emergency room, he asks Sofia, "Why am I here on this bed in this terrible place? I thought it was you who needed help."

Sofia comes close to him and holds his hand. She assures him that everything will be fine.

"I need to speak with Juliana right away," he says. "I'm alarmed about the project. Have you talked with Maigret? Have you heard from Marina? Is she OK?"

Sofia doesn't grasp anything he's saying. She calls for the nurse to give him something to sedate him or at least calm him down.

The nurse returns with a strong dose of Ativan and some water. "Sir, please take this tablet. It'll make you feel better until a doctor sees you."

"Why?" he asks. "I'm fine. I think it's Sofia who isn't well." He turns to his wife. "Tell her, *amore mio*, that it's you who's unwell."

Sofia persuades him takes the tablet, and a few moments later, he's in a different zone; he's in a world unknown to anyone but to him. In this world, he thinks. He never stops thinking. For him life is but a dark comedy of sorts. He recalls how, suddenly and without warning, he discovered significant changes regarding his behavior, physique, abilities, and over-all well-being. It all started one day and progressed from then on.

Clumsiness was the first thing he noticed. He wakes up in the middle of the night as a result of insomnia and walks around his apartment not knowing what to do with himself. Shortly after, he decides a cup of cof-fee is a great idea—that is, after a few whacks of his arms, elbows, legs, toes, and several other body parts against any and all the objects in the apartment.

He goes to the kitchen and prepares the coffee; he makes it the old-fashioned way. He puts fresh water in the kettle and places it on the stove. While waiting for the water to boil, he gets his cup, places the cone he uses in the cup, and adds two spoonfuls of espresso forte to the filter inside the cone. Often he misses the filter, and the coffee flies all over the place. After a few curses, and a lot of cleaning, he goes through the process once more. Then he waits. After discovering he's waited longer than humanly possible, he checks why. He smiles as he realizes he's forgotten to turn on the stove for the water to boil.

His smile doesn't last long. After the water is ready, he pours it into the filter with the espresso coffee in it. About halfway through the endeavor, he often misjudges the distance and violently smacks the cone; the cup of coffee tips over and fresh coffee spills all over the counter, the stove, and the floor. Again, after a few curses, the long process of cleaning takes place. At times he entirely gives up on the idea of having coffee; other times he restarts the whole process again.

One morning, after he made his coffee, he pulled the milk out of the refrigerator but discovered it had expired. After a short decision-making process, he opted to go to the store for milk. He put on his shoes, got in his car, and drove the ten minutes to the store. When he returned, the old milk was on the counter next to the sink. He placed the fresh milk next to it and went to the bedroom to take off his shoes. When he came back to the kitchen and was preparing a fresh cup of coffee, he decided to pour the old milk in the sink. He calmly and swiftly did just that and waited for the water to heat up. When the coffee was ready, he poured it in the cup. Then he picked up the milk added it to his cup. He despondently discovered that he had emptied the new bottle of milk and had poured the expired milk into his cup. Ever since that incident, he hasn't added milk to his coffee. He drinks it black.

Each morning his physical appearance astounds him. He swears that his face changes on a daily basis. Black circles around the palpably wrinkled areas under his eyes attract his attention. Then, later, wrinkles around his forehead and mouth start to emerge. Soon after, he loses all his teeth, and although he spends thousands of dollars on dental implants that make him look terrific for a while, he loses the implants too, due to bone loss as a result of chemotherapy. With his toothless mouth and thin lips, his face reminds him of his grandfather when he was

eighty-seven years old, a few years before his depar-
ture to the unknown world of demise. His attractive-
ness disappears; he notices that on the streets. In the
past, young pretty girls often turned their heads to
take a glimpse of him; now they don't even see him.
Only women over seventy do.

His dexterity has changed noticeably as well.
He can barely balance his body, and he walks like a
drunken man. For him the worst of all is his sexuality, or lack thereof; he's virtually lost it all. With his
lack of testosterone, his prostate enlargement, and
his rapidly shrinking and shriveling penis, sexual
desire is now an absurdity. Nothing could give him
an erection, except perhaps a goddess from King
Solomon's entourage. Even with such a goddess,
the experience would be humiliating; his body even
refuses to produce semen, as though he depleted
it all at a younger age with his numerous sexual
escapades and flings. Now he lives his sexuality
vicariously—*du fait d'autrui*—and through the wild
memories he accumulated during his playboy years.

He wonders how Sofia endures this lack of sexual
intimacy. He wonders why his prostate keeps growing while his penis continues to shrink. No doctor

has been able to answer that. Sexual desire is practically a mission impossible; hence, sex for him is also a mission impossible.

Changes in his attitude have invaded silently too. In a Trojan horse–style attack, he becomes a different man. His socialization and social skills, his love for outings and companionship, and his desires to play and frolic are now things of the recent past. He is a recluse, a hermit, an ascetic being.

He's only in his fifties, and he abhors what has been transpiring. He recalls the great Mark Twain saying, "Age is an issue of mind over matter. If you don't mind, it doesn't matter." But he minds; he demurs very much. With his eyesight fading, his energy depleting, his sexuality disappearing, his body shrinking, and his life mere words to be written, he relates more and more to Nikita Ivanovich Panin's candid and straightforward words, "In youth the days are short and the years are long; in old age the years are short and the days long." His days have never been longer; his years have never been shorter. And that is celestial comedy indeed.

He is now almost asleep because of the Ativan but not quite. A man comes in and introduces himself as Dr. Philip Sporty. He's the psychiatrist the emergency room called upon to assess the situation. He talks with Sofia, who explains everything that has been happening. She says that her husband is intelligent and tender, and she doesn't fully comprehend theses occurrences and spells he experiences. She tells the doctor that her husband is obsessed with the idea of prosecuting God in the International Court of Justice and that he talks with and about people she doesn't know.

"I'm afraid I have to give you some very bad news," Dr. Sporty says. "I think your husband is suffering from a dangerous form of schizophrenia. We don't know how to cure the disease, but there are medications that can help manage it. Has he ever been violent in any way?"

"Not at all. He's a very calm and sweet man," she replies.

"I don't want to alarm you," Dr. Sporty says, "but people with schizophrenia can get violent at any moment without their realizing it. You need to make sure he takes his medications as prescribed, and you need to be vigilant and try to know as much as you can about his activities, whereabouts, and contacts.

I'd like to keep him in the hospital for a few days for observation, OK?"

"Yes, Doctor, sure, if it'll help him. I'll be here with him too."

"There's nothing really you can do here, but you can come visit him any time. You need to care for yourself. Go home now and rest," Dr. Sporty suggests.

Sofia's husband drifts in and out of sleep. She comes close to him and tells him that he's in good hands and that she'll come see him tomorrow, Sunday. He nods and waves at her. Sofia leaves.

Ciao, Juliana. Thank you for coming to see me. How are you, and how is the project going? Are we ready to file? Where is Maigret? he says to Juliana, whom he sees standing next to him.

What happened? Juliana asks. *As soon as I heard, I came directly to see you. I called Maigret. He'll be here soon.*

I don't know exactly what happened, he says. *Sofia brought me here, and the doctor says I'll have to stay for a few days. I have no idea why. First I thought it was Sofia who wasn't well, but I was wrong.*

Juliana softly says, *Ah! I think Sofia is posing a problem for us right now. We need to do something about that, don't you think?*

What do you mean by "posing a problem"? I don't understand.

At that moment, Maigret comes into the room, kisses Juliana on the cheeks, and asks, *How are you old man? Êtes-vous bien?*

Oui, je suis très bien, he replies

Juliana interjects, *I was just telling him that Sofia is creating a problem for us. He shouldn't be here in the hospital. We have work to do. The indictment of God, the investigation of Morsi and his terrorist group, dealing with the FBI—there are just too many things going on. We can't allow him to stay in the hospital. We need to work together.*

Oui, ma chère, Maigret agrees. *Bien sûr. We need to do something about Sofia.*

Maigret further explains that he's been in touch with Salvo Bruno, who's upset that the FBI has taken over the case because it's now a national security problem. He also stresses that he wants to get that son of a bitch Morsi and his friend, Gamal Nour-Eldeen.

Did I tell you this Nour-Eldeen guy has a long rap sheet of violations and convictions? he asks Juliana and him.

They both answer in the negative.

Listen, Morris, Juliana says. *We need to get him out of here as soon as possible.*

CHAPTER FOURTEEN:

LEAVING THE HOSPITAL

Maigret starts to disconnect all the medical instruments attached to him. *We'll get you out of here, mon ami,* he says.

They help him stand up, dress him, and walk out of the hospital without any of the staff noticing. They decide that Maigret will drive him away while Juliana drives her car behind them.

He is still under the effect of medications and isn't very coherent. A short while later, they arrive at Juliana's place, and he immediately looks for Sofia.

Sofia must be at your apartment, Juliana tells him.

Oh, I thought we moved here for a few days for safety after what happened to the front door, he says.

Well, she must have returned to your apartment. Juliana doesn't want to tell him that Sofia never came.

We need to have a serious conversation regarding Sofia, Maigret says firmly.

He and Maigret sit at the kitchen table while Juliana makes coffee.

Listen, mon ami, Maigret tells him in a grave tone. *Sofia is now a threat to us and our mission. We need to get rid of her. You must kill her. We really have no choice. She thinks you're hallucinating and doesn't take your conviction to prosecute God seriously. For us to succeed in our mission, Sofia has to be out of the way. She's become a serious obstacle.*

Yes, he says. *I don't understand why she took me to the hospital and left me there. It's as though she wanted to prevent me from doing what I'm doing. Or perhaps she wants to eliminate me. Yes, she's a danger to all of us. Yes, yes, yes. I must take care of her once and for all so that all our efforts won't be in vein.* He pauses for a moment then adds, *Just her friendship alone with that Marina girl and her Muslim husband is a clear sign that she's working against us.*

Absolutely, Juliana says, as she pours coffee for each of them. *Sugar or milk?* she asks him.

No, thanks, he says. *I drink my coffee black now. It's a long story.*

Maigret starts planning. He tells both of them what they have to do. He explains to him that he should go back home to his apartment in the morning. Sofia will be there.

Greet her normally, he says. *She'll certainly be surprised to see you, since you're supposed to be at the hospital. Put her at ease, and tell her that Dr. Sporty released and that you took a taxi home. Take this knife with you, but hide it carefully.*

Maigret hands him a razor-sharp Bowie knife.

Try to distract her somehow, he says. *Then attack her. Plunge the knife into her heart once. Our problem will be over once and for all. Juliana and I will be waiting for you in the parking lot. Once you're sure she's dead, bring the knife with you and come down, and we'll drive to Juliana's place. Is that clear?*

He nods.

We also need to be sure no one sees you going in or out of the apartment, Maigret stresses.

He's listening to everything and sipping his coffee, and he's in one of his psychotic states. He tells Juliana and Maigret he's very tired and should go to bed. He says good night, leaves the table, and heads to Juliana's guestroom.

He lies in bed with his eyes wide open and his mind in a whirl. He sinks into deep thoughts. "Perhaps I died," he mumbles to himself as he dives into a trance, wondering about time and life and what has transpired with Juliana, Maigret, and Sofia. He has passed life's milestone age of fifty, and he isn't too happy about it. "What!" he regularly exclaims and bellows. He doesn't know why he thinks he's dead. He knows that he remembers only one thing, and it's that he remembers nothing. To him, if there is no memory, there is no life. If he remembers nothing, he must be dead. He doesn't know whether the dead know they're dead; he wonders about that. If he knows he's dead, then he isn't dead. He isn't sure. He also isn't sure how he remembers that he doesn't remember. It's bizarre. The whole episode is eerie.

He's a few years above fifty; when pessimistic he thinks he's half a score to sixty, a score away from eighty. A score is an eye blink; he has blinked only two times so far; he thinks if he isn't dead, he has less than one blink to be. He tries not to blink as he remembers Horace's code, "*Carpe diem quam minimum credula postero.*" He waits for the miracle to come—for him to remember.

He sinks back into the past, more than twenty years ago. He picks up the phone and unconsciously dials her number.

Hello, she says.

Oh! This voice is familiar. Who might this be? he asks, as he tries to remember whom he called.

Hello, she says again.

Hello, Sofia. Is that really you? he nervously utters. *I hope I'm not interrupting anything. I've been thinking of you.*

Oh, my God! No! Not at all. This is strange, because I've been thinking about you too. Oh, my God, it's been ages, Sofia enthusiastically says.

Yes, it sure has, he replies.

Sofia is the protagonist of the most vivacious chapter in the narrative of his life. They've been in love and share the most sensuous moments, which he craves to repeat. She is an Italian, sixteen or seventeen years his junior. She's a very pretty young girl with a model-like physique and large inviting brown eyes in which he sails often with no knowledge of navigation. Lovemaking has always been a trip to the Renaissance, the remnants of which stay with him for days; it always has been an experience serenaded by angels and mermaids. He never forgets this. He worships and adores Sofia.

How can he kill her? He's back into the *now* for a fraction of a second.

He doesn't remember why he called her. There's a moment of silence between them; she finally interrupts it. *Are you still living at the same place?*

Yes, indeed I am, Sofia, he replies, and hopes he remembers why he called her. While trying to recount the moments before calling her, he takes another sip of his Cabernet Sauvignon and feels intoxicated, not with the wine but with the memories of his beautiful Sofia.

Now a miracle would be appreciated, he thinks. *I need a miracle. I don't know why I called her. What will I say?*

He hopes for a miracle to come. And he is sipping it now. For him the taste of wine is like the taste of kissing a beautiful woman for the first time; it is somewhat erotic, somewhat sensual. Perhaps in his solitude it is intensified. He is in solitude; it is intensified.

How can I kill the one love I've experienced in my life? he asks himself. *Are Juliana and Maigret correct in their suspicions? Is it possible that Sofia is jeopardizing my life?* He wonders all this but resigns to Maigret and Julian's suggestions and advice. *No, no, I must kill her. After all, they've helped me through this whole process.*

It's 4:15 a.m., and he hasn't slept yet. Or perhaps he did but doesn't realize it. He never knows. This has become his way of life; he's always in the middle, on the fine line that separates reality from fantasy and make-believe.

He finally decides he isn't going through with the plan to murder Sofia. He gets up and walks into Juliana's bedroom; she's now in a deep sleep next to Maigret. He wakes them up.

I'm not going to do it, he says firmly. *I simply can't. I can't kill my beautiful wife. I love her too much to do her any harm.*

Half asleep, half awake, Juliana tells him not to worry; she or Maigret will do it for him. He doesn't even have to be there. She tries to reason with him and explains how dangerous Sofia is to them now. She convinces him that Sofia doesn't want to bring God to justice and that she's probably in cahoots and conspiring with the Muslim guy, Morsi, and his wife

Marina. He thinks for a minute, and without saying a word, he leaves the bedroom.

He goes back to his room, where he lies in bed and suddenly suffers a seizure. He convulses and loses consciousness. As he opens his eyes and enters a state of semi consciousness, he thinks of what Juliana said.

In cahoots with the Muslim guy, Morsi? Conspiring against me? he slurs, but only he can hear the words. *Is it possible that Sofia is having an affair with Morsi?*

Suddenly he sees Juliana sitting on the corner of the bed. She talks to him quietly and tells him how much she cares for him, as he also should do for himself. She reminds him that Marina, Morsi's wife, is having an affair. She asks him if it's possible that Sofia is also having an affair. She stresses to him that all things are mere possibilities. He continues to move deeper into the dark side of his mind.

She asks him if he ever reminisces about the story of Laura and Ada, two of Sofia's friends. Suddenly he tells her the unique tale that Sofia shared with him not long ago, a story about her two gorgeous married friends, Ada and Laura. Ada is a lovely young wife with a delicate demeanor that makes her eyes sparkle under any form of light. One day she was in her kitchen in the late morning, preparing lunch. Her phone rang and startled her. Although her hands were busy chopping vegetables, she managed to pick up the phone, place it on her left shoulder, and tilt her head a bit so she could talk while chopping.

"Hello, Laura," she said. "How are you?"

"Ada, are you busy?"

"Not really. I'm just preparing lunch. What's on your mind?"

"Listen, Ada. Meet me for lunch," Laura said through her tears. "It's very important. I need to talk to you...I need to talk to someone."

"What's wrong? Calm down. Where do you want me to meet you?"

"Meet me at the Sky Room in Long Beach in forty-five minutes."

Ada called a cab then nervously tidied up the kitchen and rushed to the bathroom to freshen up. After throwing on a sweater and putting on her shoes, she exited her apartment and took a taxi to the restaurant.

Her friend, Laura, also took a taxi to the restaurant. As the driver took the ramp to Long Beach, she pulled something out of a box in her hand; she examined the items with a deep sigh and heavy tears, and hastily placed the items back in box.

The taxi driver noticed her from the rearview mirror. "Are you OK, ma'am?"

"Yes, yes, I am. Thank you."

"Would you like me to stop anywhere?"

"No, just drive to the Sky Room, please."

"Sure, ma'am," the driver said. A short while later, he pulled up to the restaurant. "Here we are, ma'am."

"Thank you. Here you are." She paid the fare and grabbed her purse and the white box and exited the taxi. When she entered the restaurant, she saw Ada sitting at a table in the corner and approached her. Ada stood up and hugged Laura, and they both sat down.

"Oh, God. Oh, God," Laura said. "You won't believe this."

She opened the white box and took out a pink bra that looked seductive in an Italian way. Then she pulled out a matching pink—and even sexier—pair of panties and held them up to show Ada.

"What's that?" Ada nervously asked.

"I received this box from Trump International Hotel with a note." She pulled out a card with the hotel logo printed on it. "Listen, Ada. 'Dear Mr. and Mrs. Lorenzo Nardonne: We found that you left these items in your room. We hope you enjoyed your stay, and we look forward to serving you again. Management.' "

A waiter looked a bit dazed as he saw Laura holding the lingerie. He pretended not to notice and placed two glasses of water on the table. Another waiter approached with wide eyes and couldn't resist looking at the sexy pink bra and panties. He clumsily placed a basket of bread on the table and almost knocked over the water glasses, but he caught them rapidly, saving himself the embarrassment.

Ada was in shock, her cheeks burning red, her hands trembling. She extended her hand to touch the bra Laura was holding. She wished the earth would open up and swallow her.

"This has to be a mistake, Laura. I can't believe it. It can't be Lorenzo. It's impossible."

A well-dressed server approached the table, greeted Ada and Laura, and asked if they wanted drinks. Simultaneously they both asked for martinis.

"Have you talked to Lorenzo about it?" Ada asked. "I mean, did you ask him about the package?"

"No, I didn't. You're the first one I called. I'm not sure what to do. What am I going to do, Ada?" Laura pulled out a handkerchief to dry her uncontrollable tears. "What am I going to do?" she repeated.

Ada couldn't hide her nervousness and distraction. "Just calm down," she said. "I'll be back in a few minutes."

She excused herself to go freshen up, took her purse, and walked away, feeling faint. She entered a stall in the ladies' room, pulled out her cell phone, and dialed a number while nervously tapping her feet on the floor.

"Come on! Come on! Answer the bloody phone."

In the dining room, Laura heard the ringing of a phone nearby and grew irritable, thinking how discourteous people are, having their ringers on so loudly in a restaurant. She turned her head toward the sound but identified nothing in particular.

"Hello, Lorenzo?" Ada said. "I'm here at the Sky Room with Laura. We're in a mess now. She knows about us."

"The Sky Room!" He nervously scanned the restaurant. "What's going on?"

Lorenzo was sitting at a table with Adrian, Ada's husband. He was very careful not to let him know Ada was on the other end. When Ada had said she was at the Sky Room, his body had turned cold, and sweat covered his forehead.

Ada proceeded to recount the events to Lorenzo.

"Don't worry. Calm down. We'll think of something," Lorenzo told her.

"Where are you now?" Ada asked.

Lorenzo showed some apprehension, as Adrian was listening. "I'm with my friend Adrian," he said, "having lunch on Pine Avenue."

"Adrian! Why? What's going on? You're not confessing, are you? Please don't, Lorenzo...Don't be stupid."

"Oh, no, no. Don't worry," he said. "How about dinner tonight? We'll talk about it then. How about we meet at the usual place at six thirty?"

"OK," Ada said. "I'll see you then."

"*Ciao* for now. See you later."

After hanging up, he explained to Adrian that the call was from a client who was having some concerns. Then he proceeded to explain to Adrian how he found a love letter addressed to his wife, Laura.

"Her car was blocking mine, and I had to return to the office on an urgent matter. I asked her to move her car, but she was busy doing something. She said the car keys were in her purse and asked that I move the car myself. When I opened the purse to take the keys, I found a folded blue letter that made me curious, so I opened it. It was a letter to Laura. I read it and put it back where it was."

Adrian stiffened and pulled his right hand up to his neck and fretfully pretended to be leveling down his hair. "What was in the letter?" he asked nervously.

" 'My darling Laura, that was the best sex I've ever had. You are so, so, so sexy. I can't wait to do that again soon. How about next Thursday, same place, same time? Let me know. Love, A.' "

Adrian was unable to control his shaking hands and knees. He couldn't find any words to say to Lorenzo. A tremendous sense of guilt came upon him like an avalanche. He took a large gulp of his red wine and stood up to go to the men's room.

"Are you not feeling well?" Lorenzo asked him.

"I'm OK. I'll be right back."

He headed toward the other end of the restaurant. Lorenzo was alone in deep thought, slowly sipping his wine. Suddenly he heard a phone ringing at nearby table.

That's the same ringtone as Laura's phone, he thought. He made nothing of it and continued to sip his wine.

Laura answered her phone. "Jesus!" she gasped. "I should have been more careful. Well, OK, see you at six thirty then. Thanks. Bye." She hung up and apologized to Ada. "It was my dentist. They changed my appointment to six-thirty tonight."

Ada gave her a perplexed look.

"Listen," Laura said. "We'll talk about this again. I'll call you soon. I'm not sure what I'm going to do, but I have to go home now. Thank you for being a good friend."

They both exited the restaurant, and each stood on the curb, waiting for a taxi. From a distance, Laura saw a man who bore a resemblance to her husband; her heart sunk for a moment, and she pointed to the man and said to Ada, "He looks a lot like Lorenzo, doesn't he?"

They both ignored the thought; each of them got into a taxi and waved good-bye.

At 6:20 p.m., Adrian showed at La Triviata, and Laura appeared a few minutes later. They greeted each other and waited for the hostess. Suddenly their faces looked haunted and sullen; Ada and Lorenzo mysteriously had materialized next to them.

When he finishes telling the tale, Juliana stresses that he should consider that story and not remain as passive and stupid as he appears to be.

Now he's very deep in that dark corner in his mind. He's thinking of murdering his wife and starts to count the reasons he must do it. Juliana is abetting him. She asks that he consider Sofia's motivations for taking him to the hospital. She assures him he is well and has no health problems; she also emphasizes what she and Maigret have done for him and says they'll always protect him.

He finally gets a moment of sleep, but it's repeatedly interrupted by incoherent and unrelated thoughts. This is just a normal thing for him now.

CHAPTER FIFTEEN:

HOMICIDE

I t's Sunday, early morning. Sofia is at home, making coffee and getting ready to go to the hospital to see her husband. She prays that he's better and no longer hallucinating.

She hopes Dr. Sporty started him on his new medication. She trusts the doctor and is confident he'll help her husband. She's completely oblivious to what is about to happen. She drinks her coffee and prepares to take a shower.

He, Juliana, and Maigret are on their way to the apartment to carry out their sinister plan. He's driving recklessly and listening to words of encouragement and comfort from both Juliana and Maigret. The whole time he holds and examines the Bowie knife Maigret has given him. He looks at it for a moment, then puts it on the seat between his legs, then picks it up again. He senses he isn't himself, but then again he hasn't been himself for a long while now.

Abruptly he asks Juliana about the complaint and the brief. He's quite desperate to know for certain that the court will accept and address the case. Juliana assures him that the matter is a done deal and that she's beyond certain that God will be tried and convicted. He smiles widely and feels a sense of victory.

Finally the truth will be out, and the world will know how savage the being they believe in as God really is, he enthusiastically declares.

He parks his car in front of the apartment building where he and Sofia live. Before he gets out of the car, he puts the knife in his trousers pocket. They enter the apartment, and he slowly opens the door, taking all precautionary measures to be quiet and not to be seen.

When they enter the apartment, they hear the noise of the shower in the bathroom. Maigret explains that now is the perfect time to kill her, as she's in the shower.

Yes, do it now, Juliana says, *before we lose this whole project.*

He's nervous and shaking. As he approaches the bathroom, he turns around. He hands the knife to Juliana and tells her he simply can't do it and won't do it. Maigret's urging, inducements, and pledges fail to sway him to enter that bathroom.

Damn it, Juliana whispers in an angry voice. *Maigret or I will do it.*

A short argument ensues between Juliana and Maigret as to who should go into the bathroom and silence Sofia forever. Juliana is decisively persuaded that she'll have to do it herself. She takes the sharp knife from the quivering hand of Sofia's husband. There's some resistance from him, but ultimately he lets go of it.

Juliana slowly enters the bathroom slowly, slides opens the shower door, and surprises Sofia.

"How did you get out of the hospital, *amore mio?*" Sofia asks. "Did Dr. Sporty release you? I was just getting ready to go to the hospital to see you, *amore mio.*"

Juliana suddenly and mercilessly plunges the sharp knife into Sofia's abdomen.

"Why, *amore mio*? Why?"

Sofia shrieks and struggles to get out of the shower, but Juliana mercilessly slits Sofia's throat. Sofia falls in the bathtub, and Juliana continues to stab her repeatedly.

He hears Sofia's cries for help, but he stands there paralyzed and with no feeling or expressions. It's as though he isn't even there.

Blood splashes everywhere. Sofia lies peacefully dead in the bathtub, and Juliana's face, hands, and clothes are all stained with fresh blood that drips to the floor as she walks out of the bathroom.

Mission accomplished. Now we go back to work and prepare for the trial, she says coldly.

Meanwhile Maigret makes a mess in the apartment. He throws papers all over the floor; he bashes any table or chair he sees; he breaks any item he puts his hands on; and he places the couch on its backside. He makes a wreck out of the apartment. He wants to make sure Sofia's murder appears to be a result of a burglary attempt or home invasion. The last thing he does is break the balcony's glass door.

Neighbors hear the commotion and call the police for help. Shortly after, he hears sirens sounds coming from everywhere. He shakes his head violently and crawls into the bathtub. He holds Sofia and cries uncontrollably.

The police knock loudly on the door, but there's no response. They resort to breaking the front door down and enter the apartment. They notice the wreck and realize a great deal of violence has occurred here.

With their guns drawn, two police officers follow the fresh bloodstains all over the apartment and enter the bathroom. They see the gruesome sight of Sofia's body being held by her husband, who is distraught, sobbing, and talking but making no coherent statements.

One of the officers calls the station and asks for homicide, forensics, and a medical examiner. Another officer can't handle the scene and runs outside. Others enter the bathroom and help him out of there. They notice he's holding a bloody Bowie knife in his hands. One of the officers puts on a pair of gloves, approaches him cautiously with his gun drawn, slowly takes the knife away from him, and places it in a plastic evidence bag.

He has blood all over his face, hands, and untidy clothes. The officer asks that he sit at the kitchen table; it's the only table that isn't overturned. On his way from the bathroom to the table, blood drips all over the floor.

Now the forensics staff is in the apartment. Two detectives from the Long Beach Police Department arrive, followed by the medical examiner. Detective Heidi Kemble is a stern, experienced, and strong-willed detective in her midthirties. Detective Mica Bauer, in his midforties, is known to be tough and persistent and has an extraordinary talent for observation.

The medical examiner, Dr. Robinson Schwartz, is a well-respected scientist whose ability to notice minute details renders him a genius. He's in his late sixties, elegant, and radiates confidence.

Police officers are taking many photographs, while the two detectives scan the premises looking for clues. A fingerprint expert is collecting evidence. Other officers cordon off the entire apartment building with yellow crime-scene tape.

Detective Bauer comes across a manuscript on the floor titled *The Indictment of God* and kneels to examine the document; he puts a pair of gloves on, picks up the manuscript, and opens it. He reads a list of verses from various religious books. He sees various names. He takes the document, places it in a plastic bag, and shows it to his partner, Detective Kemble.

While Dr. Schwartz is in the bathroom examining Sofia's body, Detectives Kemble and Bauer pull up chairs and sit next to Sofia's husband at the kitchen table.

"Now calm down please, and tell us what exactly happened here. Would you like a glass of water?" Detective Kemble asks him.

He's sobbing and shaking uncontrollably. "She killed my beautiful wife Sofia. She killed her in cold blood. Both of them did."

"Who did?" Detective Kemble asks.

"Juliana and Maigret. Yes, they both killed her. They wanted me to do it, but I refused. I love my wife."

Detective Bauer recognizes the names from the manuscript. "Who are Juliana and Maigret?" he inquires.

"They were supposed to be my friends. They were helping me complete my project, and they protected me from Morsi and his terrorist group." Bauer also recognizes the name "Morsi" from the manuscript, but he and Detective Kemble are baffled and not quite sure what they're facing here.

They see Dr. Schwartz leave the bathroom. They excuse themselves for a moment and ask Sofia's husband to stay seated until they return.

"We have a violent stab wound to the abdomen, a slitting of the throat, and several stab wounds to the body. There was little struggle. She must have been taken by surprise and known her killer. It probably have took her about ten to fifteen minutes to expire. The wounds are fresh, which indicates that the attack happened within the last hour. I'll know more when we take the body to the lab."

The doctor and the detectives order the removal of the body to the lab for a complete autopsy. Staff members of the Long Beach Police Department place Sofia's body on a stretcher, cover her with a white sheet, take her to their van, and drive off.

In the meantime officers are still collecting evidence, taking pictures, and hunting for fingerprints. They collect numerous papers, newspaper articles, and computer printouts. They also remove the computer and take all materials to the lab at the station.

Detectives Kemble and Bauer head back to the kitchen, where Sofia's husband is still sitting, sobbing and confused. The detectives open their notepads and resume their questioning.

"Tell us everything you know," Bauer says.

He starts by telling them the whole story of his wanting to bring God to justice and prosecute him in the International Court of Justice. He tells them that his lawyer friend, Juliana Maigret, was helping him draft the complaint and the brief. He relays the story of Morris Maigret's involvement and mentions Detective Salvo Bruno as well as Morsi and his wife Marina.

Then he details how his door was defaced with the phrase "blasfemous basterds." He talks about Detective Bruno's investigation as well as Detective Raul Del Rio of the Anaheim Police Department and his success in tracking down a man by the name of Gamal Nour-Eldeen, an associate of Morsi Sheikh Ahmad. He explains that Salvo and Del Rio discovered that Gamal Nour-Eldeen was running his terrorist activities from a motel in Anaheim; he adds details about the piece of paper Detective Morris Maigret found after the defacing of the front door. He explains that both Nour-Eldeen and Morsi are involved in terrorist activities and says that the FBI took the case because it was a national security matter. He finishes by stating that Juliana has completed the complaint and the brief against God and is about to present it to the court.

Detectives Bauer and Kemble look at each other in amazement. Each asks the other if they have all the information on paper now. They affirm that they both do.

They ask him if he has any relatives to stay with for now because he has to leave the apartment. He tells them he has a sister, Savanna, who lives in Los Alamitos and gives them her address and phone number. Detective Kemble picks up her cell phone and calls the number.

"Hello, may I speak with Savanna, please? This is Detective Heidi Kemble from the Long Beach Police Department."

"This is Savanna. How can I help you?' Savanna replies.

"Sorry to bother you, ma'am, but we have a situation here with your brother. I can't explain right now, but we suggest that he stay with you for a few days. Can we bring him over?"

"Yes, of course. I hope he's OK. Is he?" Savanna asks anxiously.

"Yes, yes. But something dreadful has happened. We'll tell you when we arrive. OK?" Detective Kemble says.

"OK. Will you bring him over now?"

"Yes, we'll be on our way shortly," the detective assures her.

The two detectives and a uniformed police officer drive him to Los Alamitos, where Savanna lives. They all exit the car and find Savanna waiting anxiously at the front door of her home.

She runs and hugs her visibly disturbed brother, and they all enter the house.

"Ma'am," Detective Bauer begins, "I'm afraid we have some disturbing news. Your sister-in-law, Sofia Di Marco, has been murdered, and we need your brother to stay here for a while.

Detective Kemble interjects, "Please make sure he remains in the house. We'll be in touch soon. Here's my card. Please call us if you learn anything about the incident."

The detectives and the police officer leave for the station. Savanna is crying and hugs her brother as she expresses her sympathy. He, on the other hand, isn't in the sphere of existence. He sits there with a smile and a tear, a laugh and a cry, attentiveness, absence, and distinct detachment. He tells Savanna that he wants to call their father. Savanna is perplexed and tells him their father died more than five years ago. He doesn't pay any attention to her disbelief.

In the realm generated in that dark side of his mind, he ruminates; he wants to phone his father like he used to do. He doesn't have his current number; he doesn't have his address. His father is dead. Why is he reaching for his cell phone and trying to call him?

"I don't understand, but neither do you, my dear baby sister, Savanna," he mumbles.

He picks up the phone and dials the number he still has saved on his cell phone. Each time he does so, he hears a recorded message that says, "The number you have reached has been disconnected or is no longer in service. Please check the number and dial again."

He checks the number and dials again, but he gets the same message. He still wants to phone his dad. The message doesn't say that he's dead; the message doesn't say that *he* is disconnected or no longer in service. He tries again.

All his trying is in vain, yet he still tries. Why does he try? He isn't sure why he tries, but he desperately wants to speak with his father. He calls the operator. "Operator, I've been trying to call my father for some time now, and I just can't get through," he says.

The operator tries the number while he's with her on the phone. They both hear the same recorded message, "The number you have reached has been disconnected or is no longer in service. Please check the number and dial again."

"Sorry sir," the operator says. "The number is incorrect."

He checks the number and dials again. This time he dials in his head with no phone in his hand. "Oh, good! Finally!" he bellows breathlessly. "Hello, Dad? It's me, your son." Only silence is on the other end. "Hello! Hello! Dad?" he repeats many times.

He hears a very loud voice. It's like a thunderstorm. It's like a bomb. It's like his dad's voice.

I am dead, son. I am dead, the voice says.

"I know. I know. I just wanted to hear your voice," he says.

He hangs up and smokes a pack of Dunhill cigarettes. He drinks a bottle of Courvoisier, his dad's favorite. He tells Savanna, who witnessed the whole episode in incredulity and disbelief, "Good night, baby sis." Then he gets up and goes to sleep.

CHAPTER SIXTEEN:

THE REAL INVESTIGATION

I t's early Monday morning at the Long Beach Police Department. Detectives Heidi Kemble and Mica Bauer are quite busy trying to make sense of Sofia Di Marco's murder. They receive the autopsy report, which basically states what Dr. Schwartz told them at the crime scene. The cause of death was a violent stab wound to the abdomen, a slitting of the throat, and several stab wounds to the body. There was little struggle. She must have known her assailant. She must have been taken by surprise. It must have taken her about ten to fifteen minutes to expire. The wounds were fresh, which indicate that the attack happened within an hour of the discovery of the body. The doctor had nothing else to add except his assurance that there was no evidence of sexual assault and no evidence of head trauma.

The detectives now know for certain that there was no robbery. They're puzzled. They're looking for a motive. It's evident to them that the murder was with intent, but they can't find a motive. Sofia didn't have a life insurance policy. They checked her finances, and nothing irregular showed up. She was an educated woman but didn't work. Her husband is an English professor and an unexceptional writer who published a few unsuccessful books.

"There is no motive here," Kemble tells Bauer.

They investigate the husband and his background but find no criminal record of any kind. Then they examine the story he told them and the names he disclosed.

Detective Kemble calls the Los Angeles Police Department. "Hello. This is Detective Heidi Kemble from the Long Beach Police Department. May I speak with Detective Salvo Bruno, please?"

She's confounded to hear that there is no detective by that name with the LAPD.

She asks, "Do you have any records of a vandalism incident that took place in Long Beach on June third or fourth that involved the defacing of the front door of an apartment?"

The person on the other end puts her on hold for a few minutes to check the records. She comes back with the mystifying information. "No, Detective Kemble. There's no record here of such an incident."

Stunned, Detective Kemble thanks her and hangs up.

Meanwhile, Detective Bauer calls the Anaheim Police Department to ask for Detective Raul Del Rio. He's disconcerted when he discovers there is no such detective. He shares this information with Kemble.

"Salvo Bruno doesn't exist either," she grumbles. "What the fuck do we have here? This is very weird, Mica."

Detective Bauer asks her to check on Marina and Morsi, but all searches for "Marina Sheikh Ahmad" and "Morsi Sheikh Ahmad" turn up nothing; these people don't exist either. Additionally Gamal Nour-Eldeen doesn't exist. Detectives Kemble and Bauer begin to put the pieces together and start to think that Sofia Di Marco's husband might be schizophrenic.

Detective Kemble calls Savanna. "Hello, is this Savanna?" she asks.

"Yes."

"This is Detective Heidi Kemble. We met last night. May I ask you a question?" she pauses for a moment then asks, "Does your brother suffer from any mental illness, for example schizophrenia?"

"All my family thinks so, but he's never been formally diagnosed. I'm not sure, but he certainly isn't well. He had a phone conversation last night with my Dad, who died more than five years ago."

"I see. Well, thank you. We'll be in touch with you soon. Is he at the house?"

"Yes, he's here," Savana says.

"Please keep an eye on him, and don't allow him to leave. If he becomes violent, call us immediately, OK?"

After hanging up the phone, Detective Kemble shares this new information with Bauer.

Their next move is to check hospitals in the area and see whether Sofia's husband has ever been admitted. They share the task, and each calls some hospitals. They call Long Beach Memorial Hospital, Los Alamitos Hospital, Long Beach Community Hospital, and Hoag Hospital. They have no luck so far.

While Kemble and Bauer are in the break room getting coffee, an young police officer named Marisela de la Cruz overhears them talking. "Have you guys checked the emergency rooms? It's possible that he was in an emergency room but was never admitted." They look at each other and hustle back to their desks.

They both call the hospitals again, trying to find if Sofia's husband was ever in an emergency room. Kemble calls Long Beach Memorial Hospital. A nurse receives the call, and Dr. Philip Sporty, who's standing next to her, overhears the conversation.

"The patient was here in the emergency room," he interrupts, "and I was going through the admissions process, but he escaped from the hospital."

The nurse informs Detective Kemble that the patient was there and that they have his records. The nurse says she can't give them any further information because of the strict medical-privacy laws.

Both Detectives Kemble and Bauer persuade the district attorney's office to request a court order and a judge's signature to obtain those records.

Shortly after they receive the order, they drive to the hospital and meet with Dr. Sporty. The doctor

tells them he diagnosed the patient as a schizophrenic and warned the patient's wife, Sofia Di
Marco, that he could get violent at any moment. He
added that he was in the process of admitting him
to the hospital. The doctor can't explain how the
patient left the hospital.

Kemble and Bauer thank the doctor, take the
information with them, and return to the office
to sort all this out. As they're driving back to the
station, neither of them feels like talking. They're
dumbfounded and speechless.

They arrive at the station and go to Detective
Bauer's office, where they get some coffee and recap
all the evidence.

Detective Kemble begins. "OK, we have no clear
motive. The intent isn't well defined either. We now
know that all the names he gave us are fictitious.
We have no Marina, no Morsi, no Salvo Bruno, no
Raul Del Rio, no Juliana or Morris Maigret. They're
all figments of the dark side of his mind. We also
checked with the FBI, and they have no records of
any of involvement with the terrorist case he mentioned. We now know he's been diagnosed with schizophrenia, and we have his medical records. He was

the one holding the knife. Forensic analysis shows no other fingerprints on the knife or in the apartment but his. His notes show his fears of persecution because of his attempt to bring God to justice before an international tribunal. So the motive may have been a sense of threat that Sofia Di Marco would jeopardize his project to bring God to justice."

She asks Bauer if he's with her so far. He assures her he's following her.

"Now we need a warrant for his arrest so we can charge him with murdering his wife," she says. "I'm not sure how this'll play out in court."

"OK," Detective Bauer says. "We take all this information to the DA's office and obtain a warrant for his arrest. I think this case is solved. This is the eeriest and creepiest case of my whole career."

It's late evening now, and there's nothing more they can do. Bauer tells Kemble to go home and relax. "As for me, I need a drink pronto," he says. "I'm going have a few drinks then hopefully sleep peacefully tonight. See you tomorrow morning, Heidi. Good night."

CHAPTER SEVENTEEN:

THE ARREST

He is at Savanna's house and is unable to sleep. He just suffered, but in silence, an epileptic attack. He survived it and is now in his semiconscious state of mind. He's unaware of what awaits him tomorrow; he doesn't know that he is a suspect and will be arrested in the morning.

He's thinking of Sofia, his beautiful wife, his very dead beautiful wife. He is entirely oblivious. He feels that all he does now is wait. As it has been for years, he waits. He waits for his doctors; he waits for his dentist. He waits. He waits for his chemotherapy; he waits for his meds. He waits for his check. That's all he has done.

What day is it today? he wonders.

His consciousness of time has grown vague. He wakes up and waits for the sun to set; when it does, he waits for it to rise. He isn't certain whether his days are long or short, yet he's confident his years are very short.

The dark side of his mind takes him back to his apartment. He picks up a book from his bookshelf; he opens it, reads a few pages, and places it on his desk, only to start reading another book, knowing he will never finish it. He waits for his concentration to improve, but it doesn't seem to. Since his youth evaporated so rapidly, his concentration has weakened, his ability to remember things has declined, and his talent to effectively enunciate his thoughts has vanished.

There is something I have to do, he thinks but doesn't recall what he must do. He waits to remember; he never does. There is always a nagging feeling that he has something to do, but he doesn't know what it is. Perhaps there is nothing. Or perhaps he is waiting for Juliana and Maigret to show up.

He lies down, only to realize he has to get up; he gets up but doesn't remember why. A revelation dictates the possible reason for his getting up—to smoke a cigarette.

Where are the bloody cigarettes?

He searches everywhere for them; just when he's about to abandon the search, he realizes the packet of Dunhills has been in his hand all along. It's now time to find a lighter, but there is no lighter to be seen because it's in his pocket. He grins, mumbles a few expletives, and waits. He isn't sure for what, but he waits. While waiting and inhaling much-needed nicotine, he thinks. He never thinks of tomorrows; he's unaware that he will be arrested tomorrow. He always thinks of yesterdays. The days make tomorrows unpleasant to contemplate. Yesterdays are fortified, for they are known and are already experienced and lived. Tomorrows are so far away; they require him to wait a long time for the sun to rise then set and rise again.

His solitude most of his life—and now at his sister's house—has made him weary. Though he isn't fully aware of his loneliness, his cognizance is reborn when he hears the doorbell rings. His trance is interrupted; he thinks it is Juliana, and he gets up to open the door. Though he sees a shadow through the glass door, once he opens it, he finds no one there. He smirks, mutters a few expletives again and waits. He still isn't sure for what, but he waits.

It was last night when he saw him again. They have become acquainted; they share a drink or two often. Their talks are kept to a minimum. They prefer to indulge in the ritual of wine drinking. He likes to listen to the stories Azrael shares with him.

You'll laugh at this one, Azrael enthusiastically interrupted the silence. *I had a visit to make at a little after three in the morning, and the man I was supposed to transport—he was only forty-two and a few months—was in a hotel room with his mistress. Actually he wasn't with her exactly; he was on top of her, all nude and happy. He had no clue as to what was about to happen. He didn't know his time was up, and he was about to have his best orgasm ever. Oh! I know where your mind is taking you now.* He chuckled. *And wouldn't you know it,* he said with a smile, *his time was up.* He sniggered somewhat noisily.

What a great way to go, he said to Azrael with a fake smile. *When you come for me—I mean, when my time is up and we part together, I hope I'll be in a similar situation. Do you decide the time, or is it assigned to you?*

Azrael ignored the question. They both dove back into their drinking in silence. The time came for them to part, and they repeated to each other, "*Au revoir.*" He wished Azrael would say "good-bye" instead of "*au revoir.*"

He often thinks of many things at the same time; his mind races like a baboon on steroids. Nothing he can do can make his mind rest or take a leave. He thinks about today and about yesterdays; he thinks and thinks, and nothing helps him stop thinking. He now thinks about how he was a man who loved women; he thinks about how he was a man who hated them. He thinks of each encounter; he thinks of each moment he has lived. He thinks of Sofia and how he met her; he thinks of the complaint against God and whether Juliana submitted it to the court.

His life projects itself upon the narrow screen of his brain in fast motion. He watches and remembers. Nothing seems to be in order; nothing seems to correlate. He ponders how writers are lonely animals, how he is a desolate creature. He lives within a terribly narrow space between keyboard strokes and his inklings. He often fabricates a larger space so he can maneuver and endure. The thoughts, hence the words, do not come to him that easily, so the exertion to grasp them is endless. He cannot breathe; neither the thoughts nor the words materialize; and he is running out of air, which is scarce in his limited space. What he breathes is the Dunhill tobacco he smokes, one cigarette after another, in an attempt to control the moment, but often with brutal failure. But memories come back as he strikes each key.

"Ah! Solitude!" he whispers. "It is the sperm that fertilizes the egg of a tale to be told. Will conception take place this night? Will it be tomorrow? Will it ever be?"

He doesn't know, so he stares at the keyboard and waits.

"Here comes a thought—no not good." He says this a thousand times, writes a few hundred words, then waits for the next thousand thoughts.

"Will I see Azrael later?" He interrupts his contemplations. "He didn't answer my question. Does he decide the time, or is the time assigned to him?"

He decides to ask again the next time he sees him. He waits for Azrael to appear and hopes that this time will also end with an "*au revoir.*"

Sadly, it is close to an "*au revoir.*" It is 8:18 a.m., and Savanna's doorbell rings. She rushes to the door before her brother does. It is the two detectives along with two uniformed officers.

"Good morning, ma'am," Kemble greets Savanna. "We have a warrant for the arrest of your brother. May we come in, please?"

Savanna breaks into tears and calls for her brother to come to the door.

"Good morning, sir," says Detective Bauer. "Officer Jacobson here will read you your Miranda rights. You're under arrest for the murder of Sofia Di Marco."

As Officer Jacobson begins to read him his rights, another uniformed officer tries to handcuff the suspect. The suspect maneuvers around the detectives and officers and starts to run. Detective Kemble, with her gun drawn, shouts, "Stop, or I'll shoot."

Detective Bauer, also with his gun drawn, shouts for him to stop.

He doesn't adhere to the warnings and continues to run without knowing why he is running. Juliana and Maigret are next to him, running and encouraging him to run faster and faster. One of the uniformed officer fires a single shot.

From a distance they see him lying facedown, motionless. They cautiously approach him while Savanna screams and cries.

The officer who fired the shot is an excellent shooter; the bullet went straight through his heart. While he's lying motionless and breathing his last moments of existence, Juliana kneels and whispers to him, *We made it. I filed the complaint and the brief with the court this morning. You made it, my friend. You got God to stand trial. All savages must face justice.*

He smiles and recalls his visit with Azrael when he said, *I had a visit to make at a little after three in the morning, and the man I was supposed to transport—he was only forty-two and a few months—was in a hotel room with his mistress. Actually he wasn't with her exactly; he was on top of her, all nude and happy. He had no clue as to what was about to happen. He didn't know his time was up, and he was ready to have his best orgasm ever. Oh! I know where your mind is taking you now. And wouldn't you know it, his time was up.*

That was then. Now he is alone, without Sofia. Four police officers and many curious passersby surround him. He closes his eyes and sees Azrael, and they depart to the unknown world, where his father and brother and friends have been for a while.

EPILOGUE

The Long Beach Police Department works on sorting out the shooting and the whole affair. It isn't an easy task for them; there's not much more for them to learn. He's dead. His body goes to the coroner for an autopsy.

The uniformed officer who fired the fatal shot is put on administrative leave, pending an investigation. It was clear that the man wasn't armed, and the two detectives, Heidi Kemble and Mica Bauer, knew he was a mental patient.

Even though he made it clear to his family and friends that his body should go to scientific research when he died, his family, being Christian Copts, decide to bury him. Savanna requests that his tombstone read, HERE IS LAID TO REST A VICTIM OF THE HUMAN CONDITION.

EPILOGUE

The police eventually return all the items and documents they collected from his and Sofia's apartment to Savanna. She is distraught and in deep grief.

A few days pass, and Savanna picks up the manuscript her brother wrote. His ideas, his writing, and his mission to bring God to justice intrigue her. She finds the complaint and the brief to be convincing, compelling, and gripping. She reads the document many times, and the more she reads, the more she is absorbed and persuaded.

Savanna puts the complaint and brief in order and sits at her desk, contemplating. She finds an unusually strong impulse to continue what her brother started. She picks up the phone and shares her inclination with one of her best friends, Nathan Jenkins, a high profile attorney with extensive experience as a trial lawyer.

Nathan listens attentively to Savanna and also becomes intrigued and enthralled with the idea. He sees it feasible and, from a legal perspective, sound. He agrees to meet with her the next day.

When they meet, Savanna hands him the documents; he scans through them and is even more captivated. He tells Savanna that he will rewrite the complaint and the brief and will, indeed, submit them to the International Court of Justice.

The following Monday, Nathan has all the documents he needs and proceeds to submit the complaint to the United Nations' Office of High Commissioner for Human Rights in Geneva.

Not long after, all media organizations and networks learn of the acceptance of the complaint. The story becomes a media explosion. Everywhere one looks, newspapers, magazines, and radio and TV news networks are reporting on the unprecedented case.

Savanna is at home preparing dinner while her television is on. She suddenly hears a breaking news bulletin, in which the anchor states in a somewhat stunned voice, "The International Court of Justice has agreed to hear allegations against God. God is, indeed, on trial."

She takes a deep breath, and with a smile and a tear, she continues to cook. She pours a glass of Cabernet Sauvignon, raises it, and in a trembling voice says, "Here's to you, sweet brother."

Hollywood Book Review

Krista Schnee

For the main character of Sabri Bebawi God On Trial, each moment brings a torment of some kind. The character is extremely intelligent and yet disturbed by thoughts that never cease, as well as memories that evoke strong responses, eventually leading to a confusion of time and current reality. Indeed, as time progresses, the confusion grows worse; his reality rarely merges with truth. Paranoia and hallucinations take over his mind and thoughts, provoking dangerous responses on his part.

As this deterioration advances, his connection with his wife becomes tenuous in that she is not able to understand the dimensions of his personal reality. He may have little intellectual connection with his wife, but one portion of his thoughts remains largely coherent. In an attempt to gain some recompense for his suffering—and possibly to protect others from similar problems—he wishes to put God on trial. With little sleep or rest, he begins to gather the data needed for such a task even as his life begins to fall apart. His rage against God takes on new proportions as he develops the case; reviewing Holy Scripture, he in fact finds God culpable in the most heinous of crimes against humanity. The case envelops his imaginings, isolating him from those who care about him most.

This disturbed man is presented in Bebawi novel as a remarkably compassionate person who has experienced the worst of life in his various ailments. He is certainly representative of much of the reader's own private questionings of God and the trials that are faced by even the most innocent. Even in the midst of obvious hallucinations, he provides a lucid argument against God, definitely not the ravings of a madman.

And yet mental illness is one of his problems, the most prominent one during the action of the novel. Following his thoughts through various mental states, the writing in Bebawi book is chaotic but not confounding; it is more disconcerting in that the reader witnesses the suffering of such a kind and intelligent man in the midst of mania and delusion. Bebawi skillfully leads the reader through the meanderings of his mind and leaves the indelible impression of a man who did not deserve his fate. Too, the writing is obviously sympathetic toward those with mental illness without being condescending or overly dramatic in its representation.

By presenting the argument against God within the context of the thoughts of a mentally ill person, Bebawi may be providing a "safe" place for such discussion. Some may dismiss the case that the character is developing as that of delusion, and yet there are those in the novel who find it remarkable. Following the main character as he gathers his information from the various religious texts, the reader may make a similar conclusion. Or, if religious, he or she might simply find a common ground with this man in his suffering and the rage caused by it. Bebawi leaves such a decision up to the reader and his or her conscience.

This intricate story is so captivating with such vivid, detailed characters, that readers will fall in love with this book. Even within the space of a short novel, Sabri Bebawi is able to present difficult—and often private—questions of life, God, and reality in the harsh existence of a mentally ill man. Through smooth prose that expresses the man's desires,

Bebawi provides the reader with not necessarily the answer to whether or not God is guilty of crimes against humanity, but rather the context in which to begin answering those questions. The fictional space of the book provides only the beginning of this discussion, and yet it is a powerful beginning.